DREAMS TO SELL

Lucy Lorimer is well content, with a job in Manchester, a congenial flat-mate, Elinor, and an attractive boyfriend, Justin Wain. Then one day from an Edinburgh solicitor comes a letter telling her that she has inherited Briarybank, an old house on the Scottish Borders. She and Justin drive up to inspect her inheritance. It is assumed that she will sell it, and the Laird of Fenton is keen to buy, Briarybank having been the Dower House of the Fenton estates and the original home of the centuries-old Fenton family. But seeing Briarybank and the romantic Border country triggers off old memories for Lucy. She sees again a face she had once loved. A decision to sell can no longer be taken for granted.

DREAMS TO SELL

Janet Beaton

CHIVERS PRESS
BATH

First published in Great Britain 1978
by
Robert Hale Limited
This Large Print edition published by
Chivers Press
by arrangement with
Robert Hale Limited
1992

ISBN 0 7451 1674 4

© Janet Beaton 1978

British Library Cataloguing in Publication Data available

If there were dreams to sell
   What would you buy?
Some cost a passing bell;
   Some a light sigh,
That shakes from Life's fresh crown
Only a roseleaf down.
If there were dreams to sell
Merry and sad to tell,
And the crier rung the bell,
   What would you buy?

Thomas Lovell Beddoes
(1798–1851)

For Isabel Wilson,
Haddington

DREAMS TO SELL

CHAPTER ONE

Justin was already at a corner table when I got to the Bella Napoli.

'Lucy Lorimer,' he said sternly, 'you are late. Not just a little late, nor a quarter of an hour late, but one whole half-hour—'

'All right!' I flopped into the chair he had gallantly drawn out. 'I've got an excuse!'

He stood smiling down at me for a moment, before taking his seat again across the table with its cheery red-checked cloth. He was smart in a nattily-cut suit with a waist-coat. The tan he had collected on the Dalmatian coast in the summer hadn't quite gone nor the sun-bleaching from the fair hair that waved over his broad forehead. And it was a broad forehead. You noticed it, and the square thrusting jaw-line. Justin Wain was a young man you felt was going places.

'Well?'

'Well what?'

'The excuse.'

'Let's order first.'

Ordering was no problem. There was a wide choice of exotic food, but you paid.

'Pizza or pizza?' he said. 'Or pizza?'

'*Formaggio*.'

The Italian waiter corrected my

1

pronunciation, smiled in his kindly way and nodded.

'Cheese pizza.'

'I got out of school just in time to see my bus pulling away from the stop.'

'Feeble. It's a ten-minute service. Which leaves twenty minutes to talk away.'

'It began to rain just then, so that when I got to the flat—'

'You were soaked and had to have a bath!'

'I'd have had a bath anyway. My class was using poster paints this afternoon and an awful lot of the paint had got on me. No, there was a letter.'

'Ah?' The wine waiter from a signal Justin had given him brought a carafe of the cheap red wine we always drank. 'And you have inherited a fortune!'

I gazed at him. 'You haven't ever warned me that you have "the sight"!'

'"The sight"?'

'It's how they put it in Scotland—in the Highlands, anyway. The ability to *foretell*!'

'You mean—' It was his turn to stare.

'Not a fortune,' I said, 'in so many words—'

He relaxed. 'You had me worried!'

'—but near enough. I have been left a house.'

Our pizza arrived, enormous, succulent, steaming hot.

Justin filled my glass. 'What sort of house?'

I thought of my step-father's semi in N.

2

London where Justin had visited after we had all got back from Yugoslavia. Justin and I had met on the island of Korcula, two young people somewhat at a loose end, gravitating together. I had gone on holiday with my mother and my step-family more to prove no hard feelings than anything else. They hadn't liked my leaving a good job in London for a post in the bleak North-west. 'Bleak' was their word. I had found the people warm and welcoming, the surrounding country unexpectedly beautiful. And it was better to have made the break. My step-father had had me around long enough. Justin had been on his own in Korcula. His friend—I suspected female, but he had never told me—had 'had to cancel'.

'It's in the Scottish Borders. I haven't seen it since I was five. My mother and I went up there from London for a bit when my father was killed in a road accident. I remember it as a sort of castle.'

'A *castle*?'

'Well, you know what it's like when you're small. You see everything and everybody larger than life. When I see it again it will have dwarfed.'

Justin laid down his knife and fork. 'How come you inherit a castle, Lucy Lorimer?'

'It's a long story. It belonged to my grandparents—that is, my father's parents. My grandmother has just died, the lawyer said in

3

his letter. She had been ill for some time, and I didn't know. Mother can't have known. She doesn't ever keep anything to herself.' Which was a polite way of saying that my dear impulsive affectionate mother was notorious for blurting out whatever was on her mind. 'It seems so terribly hard, those two old people dying without their only grand-child knowing or caring. *They* must have cared a lot, to leave their house to me. We hadn't ever kept up, you see. They wanted us to make our home with them, mother and me, when my father died. But a few days in the country and my mother is frantic for the big city!'

'She was all right on Korcula and it's remote enough!'

'That was different. It was hot, for one thing, and she loves grilling on a beach. And there was dancing in the hotel every night. No, Briarybank with black night down and owls hooting was more than she could take, and she more or less ran back to London, dragging me with her. I would have stayed. I loved it! Of course, everybody was grief-stricken about my father—my grandparents and the people around who had known him all his life. But somehow everything seemed all right, if you know what I mean. I suppose, at five, you don't really understand—

'The grandparents wanted to keep me. They even suggested an arrangement, a kind of

4

adoption, to leave my mother free. But she wouldn't have that. And quite soon she married again. The old folks, I'm told, were scandalised at what they regarded as indecent haste. And Walter Kydd was not good enough for their son's widow and daughter.'

Justin said, 'Your pizza must be getting cold.'

It wasn't, but I gave it more attention.

'You know my mother,' I went on. 'She is generous to a fault. I believe she honestly did her best with the old Lorimers and they froze her off. She had always been a bit afraid of them. I think she had been a little afraid of my father too. Anyway, she's been so happy with Walter, and once Christopher and Corinne came they were her whole world. By the time the Lorimers had thawed a bit and might have been thankful to see her on her terms, she had moved on.'

Justin's plate was empty. 'Look, I *am* sorry! I didn't mean to bore you with my family skellingtons!'

'They're fascinating. So what happens now?'

I stuck on the last quarter of pizza. My throat was dry in spite of the red wine. 'The lawyer wants me to go up to Edinburgh to see him.'

'When will you go?'

'He said to make it as soon as possible. There are a lot of things to arrange. The letter went to London, of course, and Mother can't have

5

re-directed it straightaway.'

'What about Saturday, then, if his office is open? We could leave early.'

'*We?*'

Justin smiled. 'I'll run you up. It's a good excuse for a jaunt. We could have the night in Edinburgh and take in your castle on the way back.'

'That would be very nice.' For some reason I wasn't entirely enthusiastic. Briarybank held very special memories. But how else could the visit be done so smoothly? 'It's really very kind of you, Justin, but I don't want to impose on your good nature!'

He grinned. 'A man is happy to be imposed upon by an heiress!'

He kept up the heiress thing and it irritated me.

'Briarybank is more likely to prove a millstone round my neck than anything else,' I told him crossly as we drove north the following Saturday early. The lawyer had agreed on the telephone to see me whenever I arrived. He had sounded formal and distant and very Scottish. I was not looking forward to the interview ahead.

It was cold and blustery. Over the Lake District the sky was black. Crossing the Border I almost missed the sign. Soon we were among hills, piebald with russet bracken and blackening heather. We rose into cloud. 'I'm sorry, Justin.'

6

'Whatever for?'

'Dragging you up here. It's cheerless and cold—'

'I admit Korcula was more to my liking!'

I felt a stab of nostalgia for those golden days. The sun had blazed down from a cloudless sky on golden stone and red-tiled roofs. Against the green pines and the fringing beach the sea had been very blue. We had wandered hand-in-hand through the old town, exploring the narrow streets, sampling the cafés, watching the fishermen at their boats and the white cruise ships coming in. Justin had kissed me and told me how pretty I was and I had felt happy. It had been a self-contained little time, like an effervescent champagne bubble. Continuing our relationship now, I in my teaching job, he a pharmacologist in the Hermann Gunther Research Institute, was quite another thing. I watched him sidelong. He was in casual clothes today but even in casual things Justin was smart. I watched his hands on the wheel. I had never noticed how stub-ended his fingers were until now. Slim and elegant, he had clumsy hands. I warmed to him.

'Have you been to Edinburgh before?'

'No.'

'Nor I. Athens of the North, one of the romantic cities of the world!'

But I didn't find Edinburgh in the least romantic. Rain was coming down from low

7

tawny-coloured cloud. The city centre was busy and it was difficult to park. The famous Castle was barely visible. High buildings rose above the streets on either side like cliffs, the rain-soaked stone was dark.

Under umbrellas we searched out the office of Mr Macdonald. The street door was all shining black paint and polished brass. The actual premises were one floor up and dingy like something out of Dickens. Typewriters in the office seemed an anachronism.

Justin stayed behind in a dim little waiting-room when I was shown, still dripping, into Mr Macdonald's sanctum. He was white-haired and tall, with a dry look of brittle bone.

'Oh dear,' he said, 'but you are wet. Take off your coat, Miss Lorimer.' He helped me out of my plastic mac and hung it on mounted deer's antlers that served as a hat-stand. Then he motioned me to close in to the glowing gas fire. That, at least, was modern and entirely efficient.

I was aware of his blue eyes scrutinising me as I sat down.

'Aye. You have a look of him, of Robert Lorimer, that is, your grandfather. I never knew your father once he was grown. I remember him as a laddie at Briarybank.' The old lawyer moved his hands up and down his knees. 'Robert Lorimer loved Briarybank. He fancied himself, you know, as a Border laird, like his beloved Wattie!'

I must have looked puzzled for he said, 'Sir Walter Scott. Your grandfather was a great man for Sir Walter. But don't mistake me, my lassie, he was a clever advocate. I remember well, when I was young in the law, going to hear Robert Lorimer pleading a case. Aye!'

There was a pause. Out in the street traffic swished past. Rain pattered on the high uncurtained windows. I looked about the room. There were bookcases and filing-cabinets and everywhere papers. The walls were beige and the paint-work brown. There was a feel of dust.

'I'm so sorry—' I began, but a look in his face stopped me. Then I went on. 'I was not going to say I was so sorry my grandmother had died, but that I never saw my grandparents, apart from that visit when I was a child.'

How cold blue eyes can be! 'You knew where they were!'

To a girl of twenty that was less than fair, but he had his loyalties.

'Your mother—' He didn't go on, but he didn't have to.

'It must have been hard for her,' I said.

He inclined his head.

'My grandmother, was she in hospital at the end?'

'In hospital?' He looked shocked at the very idea. 'She died in her own bed, like your

9

grandfather three years before. Agnes Bruce saw to that.'

'Agnes Bruce?'

'Your grandparents' housekeeper. Miss Lorimer—' he hitched his chair nearer his desk—'I think we had better get down to business.'

He shuffled some papers for a moment and I saw a tremor in his hand. 'Your mother having re-married, your grandparents left to you the house of Briarybank and its contents. There is with the house some land of about ten acres. For the last few years the land has been let on a basis of yearly renewal to a Mr Purvis, a local farmer. Your grandparents have provided for their old housekeeper, Mrs Jessie Bruce, whom you may remember, and for her daughter, Miss Agnes, so that the cottage they occupy can be included in the sale of Briarybank. There is not a large amount of money. Apart from one or two bequests to charity and the provision for the Bruces, what there is comes to you. It is invested, at present, and amounts roughly to about £10,000.'

Awkward, I murmured something.

'Of the contents of the house—' He produced some typed sheets—'several articles are marked for friends: one or two pictures, a set of books—Their disposal will be taken care of. Now, as to the sale of the house—'

He leant back in his chair, finger-tips

10

together, his head cocked to one side. 'Unless you wish to give other instructions we shall be happy to act for you. Briarybank is an unusual house. Part of it dates back to the 16th century. It has been well maintained as to fabric, but it has not been modernised. A purchaser would have to spend money on it. Nevertheless, Miss Lorimer, I have reason to believe that it will readily find a purchaser. The laird of Fenton has an interest in it. Briarybank used to be the Fenton home and was developed and extended by the Fenton family from the Border keep that it originally was. It was used as the Dower House when Fenton fortunes were flourishing and the present Fenton House was built. It was when their fortunes slipped in the depression of the nineteen-twenties and Edward Fenton was selling off bits of the estate to make ends meet that your grandfather bought Briarybank and the ten acres from him.'

'And now Fenton fortunes are flourishing again—If this Mr Fenton wants to get it back?'

Mr Macdonald's face was closed. 'As to that, I could not say. Then a speculative builder in Clerkstoun has been in touch with us. Clerkstoun, you may recall, is the nearby town. He would be buying the property to secure the land. He seems confident of obtaining planning permission for the erection of executive housing. Briarybank can be regarded nowadays as within commuting distance of Edinburgh.

11

There is money in Clerkstoun from the cloth mills. Hence a demand for six-roomed houses with two bathrooms!' The lawyer smiled wryly. 'Using six acres, say, with three houses to an acre he would have eighteen houses to sell for over £30,000 a piece. You can see he could go to a high figure for Briarybank!'

Arithmetic was not my strong point but even at my pace I got to a dizzy sum.

'However,' he said, 'that would not necessarily be to your advantage. For death duties the land will be valued as for agricultural use. If it were sold for development there would have to be a revision of valuation and it could well be that what you gained on the swings you lost on the roundabouts. One way and another, with death duty paid, I think you could be certain of clearing £25,000. And whether you wish us to act for you or not, Miss Lorimer, I would advise auction as the best way of disposing of Briarybank.'

Disposing of Briarybank! As if it were something to be swept up and got rid of! Not that Mr Macdonald felt about the house in that way! He was interpreting my feelings. He was 'acting for me'.

'I would like to see the house, Mr Macdonald. Do you think that would be possible? Some time this week-end, while I am in Scotland?'

Jam it all into the shortest possible time, a

glance round the beloved house and the business visit to him! He could not hide his cold distaste.

'We might be able to get down there this afternoon,' I said, 'but that doesn't give the housekeeper much warning. Of course tomorrow being Sunday—'

'I shall arrange for you to see the house, Miss Lorimer. Would tomorrow at eleven o'clock suit you?' A flash of pleasure unexpectedly showed in his face. 'Miss Agnes will certainly plead church, but her attendance is not as regular as all that!'

Over lunch in a pub in Rose Street I told Justin as much as I could remember of what the lawyer had said.

'Death duties!' he exclaimed. 'If it weren't for that you could do a deal direct with the spec builder and you'd be rolling in the stuff!'

It wasn't a line of thought I wanted to follow. I needed comfort. Quite why I wasn't sure. It had something to do with the grandparents I had never known. For now I shrank from thought of the house. It was all too painful. I wished I hadn't arranged to see it. I wished I need never see it.

We walked along Princes Street, jostled by crowds. We climbed up a steep winding street that led to the rib of the Old Town. From here we had a sweeping view of the busy street we had come from and acres of city between it and

13

the silver band of the Firth of Forth with land beyond. Westwards I could see mountains touched with snow. Or was it cloud mottled with cold light? Justin suggested the Castle but I said, 'No.' Someday I would come back and visit the Castle. That was not for now. We wandered down the Royal Mile, gazing with other tourists at John Knox's House and the finely restored tenements that had been noble-men's houses in the time of Mary, Queen of Scots. The Palace of Holyroodhouse was like a French château, all golden stone and story-book turrets.

'I hadn't realised it was like this,' I said. My father had told me the old stories. We went round with a guided party and snatches of Scotland's history came back—the murder of Rizzio, the Queen's secretary, in front of her very eyes, the ball when Bonnie Prince Charlie was fêted en route for London and his ancestors' throne.

The wind blew sleet in our faces when we left the Palace.

Justin said, 'Give me Korcula!'

Next morning I woke to find my hotel room full of sunshine. From my window above the city sprawl I could see the Pentland Hills, their outlines hard-etched against a cloudless sky, every detail of whin bush and scree runnel clear as though seen through crystal. My depression lifted and I could hardly wait to eat breakfast.

Justin was amused. 'In a hurry to view your inheritance!'

The drive southwards was a heady joy, out of the city—romantic enough today—up from the Lowland plain to the pass over Soutra where in olden times my guide book told me a drove road had led by an ancient hospice. From the lonely hills we dropped gently by a widening valley to woods of beech all golden with autumn and shot with misty sunlight.

'Pretty!' said Justin.

I scarcely glanced at the road map. 'Left here,' I said.

The woods thinned out. I caught glimpses of houses half-hidden in rhododendrons. Sheep dotted the gently rolling hills. A ruined castle perched above a brown sparkling stream had me straining back to look.

Justin said, 'I hope yours is in better shape than that!'

And then I realised we were approaching a town. After the glorious countryside there was an unattractive stretch of road lined by drab houses and allotments with corrugated iron huts. In the town itself shops and houses stood baldly on the streets with no softening of trees or gardens. The town centre this Sunday morning had a shuttered look. Back from the shopping area were great rectangular buildings with ranks of windows.

'Cloth mills,' said Justin. 'They're on a river.'

15

'If this is Clerkstoun,' I said, 'we must have passed Briarybank.'

Justin drew into a parking place and took the map.

'Let's have a look!'

My spirits had plummeted again. This was an ugly town. 'My' house was two miles out from the town and the last two miles had been unlovely and sunless, lying under a grassy humped hill.

'It's Clerkstoun all right,' said Justin, 'but we haven't passed Briarybank. We've come in by the main road. Where you said to turn left—'

'We should have gone straight on?'

'For Briarybank, yes.'

I sat forward, my hands clenched, as Justin found his way through twisting back streets to the side road that led out to my grandparents' home. Across a narrow bridge the road began almost at once to climb. Looking back, I could see Clerkstoun below us on its snaking river. On land made almost an island by its loops stood a broken wall in red sandstone, its sole surviving window in the Gothic style with elaborate tracery.

The grassy slopes on either side of the road were screened by tall tangled hedges of thorn and bramble and wild rose, generously scattered with hips and haws. The road twisted round the hill and plunged. I gripped my seat as the car nosed down and then it levelled out. We could

16

have been moving forward in some glorious cathedral nave, with soaring beech trunks for columns and golden branches for fan vaulting, with gold from the roof scattering down and misty sunlight driving shafts in the spaces the gold pieces had left. On my right were white gates, standing open, a lichened board that read Briarybank. We had arrived.

It seems unlikely and yet it is true. Of that moment of arrival I remember hardly anything. I had an impression of a dark overgrown drive, of a wide gravel sweep and a white house front. Which of us got out of the car first, which of us rang the bell I can't remember. The door was opened by a big-boned woman in a neat grey suit. Her hair was done in a severe style, emphasising the hard lines of her face. I have no recollection of the first words Agnes Bruce said to me. She was civil but entirely without warmth or interest. She conducted us briskly round the house my grandparents had left me as though I were a casual visitor to a stately home. Not that it bore much resemblance to a stately home. It had indeed shrunk from what it had been in my child memory. Basically, a conventional two-storey house had been built at right angles to an old square keep or tower, the arms enclosing two sides of a courtyard at the back. On the ground floor the drawing-room and dining-room faced the front; at the back a morning-room or study looked on to the courtyard. Across the passage old-fashioned kitchen premises sprawled, inconveniently planned. Upstairs were five bedrooms and an antiquated bathroom. The keep, reached by a passage, and with a spiral stair leading to the upper floors, had been used mainly for storage. My overall impression was of rooms unlighted by colour made still more dim by heavy faded furnishings.

Out of doors things were no better. Just as the fabric of the house seemed in good repair, so grass was cut, hedges were trimmed. But nothing creative or constructive had been done for years. The house had grown old and tired along with its owners.

I led the way back into the hall, wishing I hadn't come. Agnes Bruce kept close on my heels, as though she didn't trust me with the bric-à-brac. And yet she had been good to my grandparents, seeing to it that they died in their own bed. Not knowing what to say, I said nothing.

Justin closed up to me. 'A touch depressing,' he said and squeezed my hand. I was grateful and smiled up at him. My castle! The utter sadness of it! And yet— The stairs were of oak, and broad. They rose to a half-landing and a window with coloured glass. The proportions of the hall were fine. I saw it for a moment with new rugs on the hardwood floor, white paint on the walls with their delicately moulded cornices.

It could be beautiful again! Old paintings hung where the stairs branched two ways to a wide gallery, some portraits, some landscapes with the patina of age and a fissure of tiny cracks.

'Do you remember anything?' Justin asked.

'Nothing.'

That was what was so wholly disconcerting. I had imagined that once I was in the house, so vividly experienced all those years ago, I would recognise something—

I turned to Agnes Bruce who stood quietly waiting for us to leave. 'I should like to go into the garden again. The wood beyond the garden—has that been let to Mr Purvis?'

'Oh no. The land he has is all to the Clerkstoun side. It's under turnip.'

Justin followed me out through the flagged back kitchen into the warm sun. 'Under turnip?'

I giggled suddenly. Reaction, release from tension, I suppose. 'The field is planted out with turnips.'

'So you speak the language, Lucy Lorimer?'

I paused in the courtyard. It had a French look. With geraniums in tubs it could be pretty.

Round the corner of the old tower, set cosily against a sheltering belt of spruce, was a cottage. White-painted like the big house, it looked bright and lived-in, as the big house did not. Smoke curled up from one of the chimneys. A large black cat stared unblinking from a sun-trap on a window-sill. Lace curtains at the window moved and before we had passed on the cobbles the front door opened. A small old woman, her grey hair in a bun, her feet in slippers, came out and unashamedly inspected us.

I smiled. This must be Jessie Bruce.

She nodded. Her face was incredibly wrinkled. Her eyes were a faded blue. Over eighty she had much more charm than her angular daughter. 'Guid morning to ye,' she said.

'Good morning, Mrs Bruce.'

'Miss Lucy.' She nodded her head again, drawing her lips in over her gums. Then she turned her attention to Justin. 'And this will be your wee bit mannie?'

Beside me Justin made a strangled sound.

'This is a friend of mine from Manchester, Mr Wain.'

Old Jessie Bruce put out a lined hand and Justin shook it with commendable gallantry.

'Aye,' she said, 'it was a sad day for us when your puir grandmother passed on. No' that she was laith to go at the end. It comes to us a' and she had a guid life. But now me and Agnes—Well, I came a bride to this wee hoose—' She turned and let her eyes go over the cottage front, with the michaelmas daisies massing purple and red in the fringe of garden. 'My man went frae here to the Great War and

20

his wee lass was born here, that he didna live to see. And Agnes lost her ain lad in the next war and just stayed on wi' me. I'd fain ha' ended my days here. But I'll be getting along in!' Bending forward, she propelled herself at a shuffle up the path and into the cottage. I realised why. Agnes had appeared round the corner of the big house.

'Come on!' muttered Justin.

We walked on quickly. An attempt to grow a few vegetables had been made in a corner of the garden, but the fruit garden had got out of hand. Raspberry canes were growing free of restraining wires. Currants and gooseberries had not been pruned. Apples hung on some of the trees and windfalls lay rotting on the long grass among the fallen leaves.

'Lord!' Justin was able to give vent to his feelings at last. 'Your wee bit mannie!'

'I'm *sorry*, Justin!' I gave way to helpless giggling.

We had slackened pace. He caught my hand and drew me against him. 'You must promise never, *never*—' he kissed me hard—'to use that against me!'

'It would depend!'

I broke away from him and ran on into the trees. Things were coming back now. It was a beech wood. I remembered the smooth bark and the grassy knolls furry with whins. There had been little clearings among the whins with

21

rabbit holes and somewhere I had had a secret place.

Justin came up behind me and grasped my shoulders.

'Haven't you seen enough, love?' he whispered into my hair. 'It's wet underfoot and my tummy's rumbling. Let's find us some lunch!'

I stood quite still. Shafts of sunlight pierced the thinning branches. The whins with a few out-of-season flowers had thickened and closed over the grassy knolls.

'There was a stream—'

If Justin sighed he kept it inaudible. I moved forward, down a dipping slope. It was there, dropping from pool to pool, with silver birches on its tumbling banks. There had been stepping-stones that led to the Shining Hill. It was flooding back now, memory of that enchanted time. It had been winter—funny how I couldn't have told until now—and the hill that rose above the wood had been white with snow or hoar frost. I had gone on expeditions solemnly equipped with a bow and arrow my grandfather had made for me, across the stream, up the Shining Hill to do battle with the Giant that guarded the Standing Stones. But I hadn't been all that consistent in my fantasies. I had been a damsel too, searching for my knight. He had been very real.

I followed the stream down. Justin

scrambling behind me gave an exasperated 'Damn!'

I stopped. He was detaching a tendril of bramble from his finely woven slacks. Our eyes met. The cross look vanished and he caught up with me again.

'You're delicious, Lucy Lorimer,' he said as he nuzzled my hair. 'All little girl and honey gold. But my feet are wet—'

'And you've drawn a thread in your pants—'

'—and I'm wanting *lunch*!'

'I know. Justin, bear with me a minute more. You see, I'm remembering things now. There were stepping-stones and from there I used to cross on to the hill—'

'All those years ago! Such a little girl—'

His arms had come round me and had me fast, his mouth came down on mine. His kiss was sweet and it disturbed me, touching old dreams, the unformed longings of a little girl fed old romantic tales. I fought free of him, dodged him and ran. He was not in the weave of my old dreams. For now I wanted to be clear of him. But it wasn't possible for anyone to have understood. He thought I was teasing him, playing with him, and as I ran darting from the stream into the trees and back again to the stream, he followed, laughing, calling my name.

I came to the stepping-stones and leapt across. Then I came up short. A strong wire fence had been put up all along the stream's

23

right-hand bank and a few yards from the crossing was a barred gate. I scrambled over it and ran at the hill-side. There was a belt of bronzed bracken and then where a path came winding round the hill the grass, bending in the mild wind, caught the sun direct and shone like polished metal. I heard Justin behind me. Careful of his trousers he was some distance back and I was glad. The air seemed to sparkle. I listened for larksong, but that would come in the spring. I heard something, however, over and above Justin's shouted banter—hoof-falls, the jingling of harness, the blowing splutter of a horse's nostrils. And as Justin reached me and caught me against him, a horseman crested the shoulder of the hill. He was dark against the sun, seeming larger than life. Incredibly it seemed as though he carried a lance, there was a glinting about his outline as though he wore armour. Absurdly I felt a shiver in my spine. Was he real? Or was he something conjured up from the forgotten treasure-store of Border tales my long-dead father had enchanted me with?

But he was real enough. Reining in his horse, he sat round at an altered angle—a man in a twentieth-century leather jacket and breeches, with a game-bag slung over one shoulder and a fishing-rod. The reality, however, held a shock of its own. I knew the face. It was strong-featured and handsome, the head proudly carried. Two furrowed lines came above the nose, between frowning brows. A cleft came down each cheek, reinforcing the set jaw. Out of total loss I remembered him. This was the face of my knight!

So much of recognition and wonder in an instant! I felt I must have been gazing at him for an age. But there was nothing charming or romantic in the moment. The man was staring down at us with unconcealed dislike.

'There is no law of trespass in Scotland,' he said in a voice with an edge to it, 'and so I cannot tell you to get off my land. But I can and do insist that you shut my gate to keep in my sheep!'

Stupidly I turned from him and, blundering against Justin, saw that the gate I had scrambled over was swinging wide. I glanced at Justin who had reddened.

'Keep your hair on.' When Justin drawled it meant that he was angry. 'There's not a single sheep in sight. And I assure you I have no intention of taking one step more than I have to in this mud-patch.'

The horseman's eyes were on me. It was as if he chose to ignore Justin.

'I'm sorry,' I said, and stumbling away I made for the gate. Justin stayed behind. I could hear his voice, but it seemed as though the rider wasn't deigning to reply. There was a snort from the horse, the jingle of harness and I heard the animal cantering off down the valley.

Justin joined me at the gate. He was flushed and breathing as though he had been running. 'Who the hell does that git think he is? The bloody lord of the bloody manor?'

'Yes.'

For it must be—the laird of Fenton, who wanted to buy Briarybank!

'So damn' well what? We're out of the feudal system now!'

'You should have shut the gate.'

'It's like I said—There isn't a sheep in sight, and *I* didn't choose to get my shoes plastered with his precious mud!'

I secured the fastening on the gate and turned towards the stepping-stones.

'You're on his side, I suppose,' he snapped. 'Landowners unite against the townie!'

'Oh, Justin!'

'The hell with it!' He thrust his hands into the pockets of his smart jacket and struck out directly to where the white walls of Briarybank showed through the trees. My 'wee bit mannie' had lost face and Justin Wain did not enjoy losing face.

I smiled ruefully as I followed him through the wood and then I stopped. In all probability I should never be here again, in this enchanted place, in the golden autumn or the tender spring when the larks would be singing above my shining hill. I should never see him again, that man who must be the laird of Fenton, who

26

in some inexplicable way had the face of my childhood hero. My real life lay elsewhere, teaching small children in a big city school. I walked on slowly, tired suddenly and without individual will. Justin paused and glanced back. He had a long drive ahead of him. He had been kind. I hurried to catch up with him.

*   *   *

The south-bound traffic on the M6 was heavy and it was late when we got back to Manchester. Justin stopped outside my flat.

'I don't know how to thank you,' I said. 'I could never have seen both the lawyer and the house all at one go without your help.'

'Don't mention it.'

'Will you come up for a coffee?' We had eaten on the motorway.

'Will Elinor be there?'

'I imagine so.'

He gave a half-grin. He hadn't fully recovered his equilibrium. He sensed, and not altogether wrongly, that my flat-mate Elinor Braidwood, did not care for him. 'We'll call it a day,' he said. 'I'll be in touch!'

Elinor had the sitting-room warm and coffee percolating. A nursery-school teacher, Elinor is kindly and at the same time a no-nonsense person. I had been with her since I had first come up from London and had appreciated her

27

ability to be easy without straying overmuch into my life before either of us was certain we wanted friendship. That we were friends now was from choice. She had been as intrigued as Justin at my inheriting a house and had also teased me.

'Come on then,' she said, settling me with coffee and biscuits, 'tell me all about your castle!'

I kicked off my shoes and toasted my toes at the gas fire.

'Harrowing, was it?'

'Not exactly. Sad though.' I gave her some account of the house and the gardens. 'Poor Justin, I don't think he enjoyed the trip all that much!'

'You didn't ask him to go.'

'It poured all day Saturday. Then today at Briarybank one or two things—Oh, I don't know. Clerkstoun is a dreary dump. All grim grey stone and mills. I wanted to give Justin a nice lunch as a kind of 'thank you' for taking me and we went to what seemed a good hotel. But it was so cheerless and shabby. The plates were cold and the food was cold and the fire in the lounge was as good as out—'

I sipped Elinor's hot coffee. 'I had a thought on the motorway. I didn't tell Justin.'

'What was that?'

'I could turn Briarybank into a hotel.'

Elinor sprawling on the rug turned to look at

28

me. 'What in the world could you know about running a hotel?'

'I could learn.'

'Expensively! It's a highly specialised business. Stick to what you know!'

'You mean, turn it into a school?'

Elinor laughed. 'Turn it into money, love! And be thankful!' She set down her cup. Normally she was an early bedder but tonight she made no move. It occurred to me that she looked tired. She wore her hair short, brushed from a point on the crown to turn in all round, Agincourt-style. She made up well, but lines at her eyes betrayed that she had left the twenties behind.

'What about you?' I asked. 'Nice week-end?'

'Quiet.' Elinor's week-ends were always quiet. She had friends from training-college days who were married with families now. I wondered if she had ever had men friends.

'I didn't mention it on Friday—you were rushing. My job is folding.'

I sat up with a jerk. '*What?*'

Elinor smiled. 'Don't get in a lather!'

'But how come?'

'Green Street Nursery is being absorbed into Norwood School. It's sensible, really—'

'When?'

'After Christmas.'

'What will you do?'

She played with the hearth-rug fringe. 'I may

take a few months' break. It's been a long stretch. Then I'll get another job.'

Sleep didn't come easily that night. I was concerned for Elinor, concerned that she hadn't told me her news on Friday. She was so alone. At a time like this even a strong person needed support and someone to listen. I worried about my grandparents, growing old in Briarybank, dying without the comfort of knowing that their only grand-child would love their house. For I did love it. So much! If only it need not be sold! I thought how it would be, in the papers and on bill-boards: 'For Auction, Country residence with ten acres of land in the Scottish Borders...' Elinor was right about the idea I had had on the motorway. I didn't know much about running a house, let alone running a hotel. But a school! Was that possible? And Elinor out of a job from Christmas... I sat up in bed, hugging my knees, wide awake with excitement. With Elinor I could do it! But Elinor was the epitome of common sense. 'Turn it into money!' she had said, and she had meant it.

I had tried to speak to my mother on the phone before going north, but without success. On the following evening I rang again and caught her in. As I had supposed she had had no news of my grandparents. They might have been dead for years.

'So they have left you the house!' Over the

30

line she sounded wistful. 'I did try, you know, Lucy.'

'I'm sure you did!'

'But they never liked me.'

'Nonsense, Mother! Nobody could dislike *you*!'

'You didn't know the old Lorimers! John was all they had. The girl never lived who would have been good enough for him, but I came very far down the scale. And to be frank, I don't know why John did ask me to marry him—'

'We *are* low in self-esteem tonight!'

'Don't laugh! This isn't a talk we should be having on the phone, but since you *have* left London—'

'Now, Mother—'

'All right! But it's true what I was trying to say. There had been someone else—in Scotland—that he really wanted. Somebody the Lorimers wanted—'

'*Who?*'

'I don't know. She went off with another man. Your father married me on the rebound—'

'*Mother!*' I wanted to shake her and to hug her. She read too many romantic novels!

'Everybody knew but me. Nobody would ever tell me.'

'*Darling!*'

'And then when John died, while they

31

wanted *you*, they didn't want me. Oh, they tried to do the decent thing. They were good and very upright people—'

I had to smile while there was a tightness in my throat.

'I ought to have gone back later. I ought to have taken you to see them. It wasn't that I was bitter or resentful—'

The very idea! My mother bitter or resentful!

'I was just too *busy*! Life has been so *full*! And now it's too *late*.'

'I met Agnes and old Jessie.'

My mother sighed. 'Jessie was a card! She adored your father. It's all so long ago!'

'Don't get upset about it, Mother!'

I heard her sniff over the line. 'I doubt if you will get much money for the house—'

'There's some land.'

'What's land up there?' She gave a gasping little giggle. 'There's so much of it!' We laughed together.

'As long as you don't sell it to the Fentons!'

'What *do* you mean?'

'They were at loggerheads, the Fentons and the Lorimers. Don't ask me why! Fenton was a dirty word!'

I hadn't expected that.

*   *   *

The days that followed were cold and damp and

32

dragged interminably. I was deeply thankful that the mid-term break was only a week away. Elinor seemed indisposed to talk further about her own situation. Justin came round and beyond a general chat about the visit he and I had made to Scotland nothing much was said about Briarybank. In due course I had a letter from the Edinburgh lawyer: 'Further to our talk on Saturday last, we await your instructions about the sale of the property...'

Elinor said, 'If I do leave Manchester you won't have to find someone to share the flat unless you specially want company. You could even afford something nicer.'

In no way did the prospect appeal to me. As the week drew to its welcome end Justin said, 'I suppose you will be going home for mid-term?'

I said, 'Yes' quickly and hated myself for lying. And then I realised I wasn't lying! I was going to Briarybank, and Briarybank was home!

Without confessing to anyone, I set off early on the Saturday morning with my suitcase. I wasn't sure why I had allowed Justin and Elinor to think I was going to my mother in London. I knew neither would have approved. Justin would have regarded the pull of Briarybank as a reflection on himself; he had not come over well there. Elinor would have seen through to what was in my mind and would have douched my romantic notions with rational argument.

Also I was not one hundred per cent certain

that I would actually go to the house. It was
easy enough to get a train to Edinburgh. From
Edinburgh I took a bus to Clerkstoun. It was
cold and crisply clear with a feel of frost. The
George Hotel had no charms for me and it took
longer than I had expected to find a reasonable
guest house in a side street. By the time I had a
quick snack in a café the sun was going down
behind the rounded Border hills.

The road out of the town was steep and I
kept pausing to look about me. There must
have been stormy weather since the previous
week-end, for many of the leaves were down
and lay now in damp darkening drifts at the
road sides and on the fields. It was very still. A
dog barked, probably miles away. The
occasional bleat of a sheep from the hills
intensified the lonely quiet. From the high
point of the road I walked more slowly. Since I
had left the town not a single car had passed.
Would I really want to live here, in this remote
silent place? Without friends for a long time
probably, for friends here would be slow in the
making. Always supposing that I could run the
house as a school. I had lain awake at nights
doing sums and in no other way could I afford it
or justify keeping it up.

I entered the cathedral of beeches. It was
dark. Something rustled among the dead leaves.
An owl hooted. All my life had been spent in
cities, among people and lighted streets, except

those long-ago six weeks. It wasn't even as though my forebears had lived here. My grandfather had been an incomer, an Edinburgh advocate who fancied himself as a Border laird.

The beeches gave way to spruce and evergreen holly. I was at the driveway to 'my' house. I walked slowly on the grass-grown crest of the drive. I had no idea of what I was going to do. I wasn't even certain that I had any right to come. Perhaps I should have notified the lawyer. I rounded the corner and stopped in surprise. A Landrover stood on the gravel sweep. The front door was open and light poured through the inner glass door from the hall. A warm light flickered and danced in the drawing-room. I could hear voices. I felt a stab of alarm. What was going on? I drew closer. It seemed that several people were moving about the room. Where was the devoted and reliable Agnes Bruce? Anger carried me forward into the light. They had seen me, those people in 'my' drawing-room. And then a man straightened from the fire-place and I saw his face in the leaping fire-light. That face, again enhanced by light, first the blazing sun, now the glow of fire. They were coming out to me. He opened the door and we stood for a long moment staring at one another. He wore a rough sweater and his thick chestnut-coloured hair was wind-blown. At his shoulder a pretty girl strained to see past him. She was in tartan trews stuffed into high socks and she wore a silly tartan cap with a pom-pom on her head. Behind him Agnes Bruce said,

'*Miss Lorimer!*'

'How do you do?' He put out his hand. 'Keith Fenton, your neighbour.'

I felt his fingers on mine, large-boned and strong. 'I didn't realise, last Sunday on the hill—'

'Would it have altered anything?'

He smiled wryly.

'I thought the Fentons and the Lorimers enjoyed a feud?'

The wry smile snapped out. 'That's ancient history, Miss Lorimer. But then—'

You've been out of touch. All the years when your grandparents were ageing and in need of you. Only now, when there are pickings to be had . . . He didn't have to put it into words. It was in his eyes.

And it hadn't been like that! It wasn't like that at all!

CHAPTER TWO

Agnes Bruce said, 'I was not expecting you.'

I had the impulse to say, 'Obviously!' but that would have been unreasonable and

36

childish.

'It's mid-term in the school where I teach. I—I wanted to see the house again.'

'Well,' Keith Fenton took charge, 'come along in!'

They drew back and I passed into the hall. Lamplight transformed the place, winking on polished brass, glowing on wood. I caught my breath when I entered the drawing-room. The dingy walls, the faded hangings were lost in the shadows. What stood out was the beauty of the room's proportions, with the sweep of the windows and the fine lines of the marble fire-place. Agnes Bruce snapped on the light and brought all the deficiencies back into sharp focus, but I had seen enough. I knew how it could be.

'Mr Fenton,' said Agnes Bruce, 'has had one of his men on the chimney stack. We've had high winds and rain this week. Now he's seen that the fire is drawing. I've been that worried about damp.'

I turned to Keith Fenton. 'That's very kind of you.'

Agnes Bruce said, 'It's no more than he has been doing for your grandfather and grandmother these many years past.'

'Yes, well—' Keith Fenton was aware of my embarrassment. 'Your luggage, Miss Lorimer— where have you left it?'

'My case? It's at Bideawee.' I had to laugh at

37

the expression on their faces. 'It's a guest house in Abbey Street—'

'A guest house? But you're staying here, surely?' He turned to Agnes Bruce. 'It wouldn't be any trouble getting a room ready.' Subtly, it wasn't a question. Agnes Bruce with complete lack of enthusiasm said, 'It would be no trouble at all.'

'Why on earth stay in Bideawee when you can stay in Briarybank? After all, it *is* your own house!'

He was putting on a bit of an act, I sensed. His pretty companion knew it too. He caught her suddenly by the arm and drew her forward to face me. 'Miss Lorimer, may I introduce my sister Sarah?'

The pert pretty little face was so unlike his. At least I would have said so until now. But under a kind of teenage effervescence there was a look of him in the eyes and at the mouth.

She thrust out a hand and shook mine warmly. 'Hello,' she said. 'It's lovely meeting you. A bit romantic, really. Your grandmother used to talk about you. She showed me some photographs she had. I always pictured you as a little girl. Silly, aren't I? May I call you Lucy?'

'I'd love you to.'

'That's great!' She turned to Agnes Bruce. 'Do put her in the Yellow Room! There's a great old cherry that comes right up to the window and when you wake up in the morning it's as if you were right up in the tree. That's going to be my room when Keith buys Briarybank—'

'*Sarah!*' Her brother's face was dark with anger and his voice like a lash. Without looking at me he said, 'With your permission I'll collect your case from the guest house—'

'But I can't possibly give you this trouble!'

'It's no trouble. Meanwhile Agnes will settle you in and get you something to eat.'

He made to march Sarah out of the room with him but she slipped the leash. 'I'll stay till you come back!' she said. His eyes held hers. She had spirit to match his. *All right*, she was telling him, *I'll watch what I say, but I'm staying*!

I was glad she stayed. With Sarah there, Agnes had no option but to follow orders. Sarah led the way to the kitchen where an old-fashioned stove had been lit and was giving out welcome heat.

'I'll make tea, Agnes, if you collect some grub!'

Agnes Bruce went out of the back door and Sarah, winking at me, put her tongue out at the receding figure.

'Sorry, I'm not behaving very well! Agnes Bruce is full of sterling qualities and was really devoted to the old Lorimers. But she gives me the absolute pip!' She filled a kettle and set it on the stove, got cups and plates out of a cupboard. 'How long are you staying?'

'I hadn't really thought. I've got a week's holiday, but—'

'Do stay the week! It's lovely here. You must come over and meet Mummy and Daddy. You'd enjoy that. Daddy's quite famous, did you know? He's an explorer—'

'An explorer?'

Sarah perched on the scrubbed deal table. 'He hasn't ever taken interest in anything to do with the estate. When Grandpa died Keith took over all that. He's a dear old thing is Keith, but terribly conscientious and responsible and hard-working. That's why Agnes thinks he's God's gift! I just hope—'

'You just hope what?'

Her lively face clouded for a moment at some unwelcome thought, but she wasn't one to brood and the sun came flashing out. 'He was mad as anything, wasn't he, at my saying that about Briarybank. But he *does* want it, terribly.'

'Why?'

Sarah looked at me with her wide eyes. 'They say there was Fenton treasure buried here, hundreds of years ago, at the time of the '45. The Fentons were Jacobites, of course! But I'm sure that's not why *he* wants to buy it back. It belonged to Fenton in the old days. He's a great one for the family and tradition, is our Keith. It was the Dower House, where the laird dumped his Mum when he got married!'

40

I had a feeling of disloyalty to him. He wouldn't have liked her indiscretions. I said, 'Do tell me about your father being an explorer.'

She was well-launched on an account of a Libyan expedition he had undertaken in the army when Agnes Bruce came back with a cloth-covered tray. She had done me proud. There was hot soup, a plate of chicken and salad and there was a bowl of fruit.

'Our own apples and pears,' she said, but I didn't feel the 'our' was intended to include me!

I enjoyed the meal. After all, I hadn't eaten properly all day. While I ate Sarah perched on the table drinking the tea she had made in a big brown pot. If she was brimming with information she was brimming with curiosity too.

'Do you like teaching? How long have you been at it? Infants? Crikey! I'd go spare!'

I said, 'What do you do?'

She hugged her knees. 'Nothing, as of now. I left school last summer. Mummy wants me to do a secretarial course, Daddy thinks nursing is nice for a girl. That's because he had a terrible accident in the South American jungle two years back and spent ages in hospital and had a fabulous time being spoiled by all the nurses. He's handsome, you see, and charming. I'm like him!'

We laughed together. I had made one friend

41

already.

'But I gather you're not sold on either?'

'No way! I want to be an explorer too.'

'That's a bit difficult, isn't it, you being a girl?'

'The sexes are supposed to be equal!'

'With the emphasis still on the "Supposed"!'

'You're right. But women *do* explore. Women have climbed Everest—'

'Your best way would be to have a skill to offer—like geological training or meteorology.'

'Which would mean years at university and by then I'd be too old!'

She stopped and I turned. Keith Fenton had opened the kitchen door.

He said, 'I've put your case in the hall.'

I got up quickly. 'That was very kind of you. I'm afraid I've caused a lot of trouble turning up like this.'

'There was no difficulty at Bideawee,' he said, 'when I explained that you were Miss Lorimer of Briarybank!'

'Oh!' I hadn't realised that there might have been awkwardness for him to deal with. 'I'm sorry!'

'For heaven's sake, stop apologising all the time! It was never a Lorimer trait!'

I looked at him, seeing in his face the pull between understandable irritation and a sense of humour. He disturbed me profoundly, with his resemblance to a remembered dream face. His glance went past me to his sister. 'Tell Agnes we're off!'

She tipped back her cap. 'I don't want to go yet. Have a cup of tea!'

'I doubt if Miss Lorimer wants strangers around any longer tonight. Find Agnes!'

Sarah slithered off the table and went stomping out. I felt intensely shy, left alone with him and more than ever aware of the darkness outside and the deep quiet. He stood beside the stove warming himself, making no attempt at small talk. Then Sarah came scampering back, blowing on her hands.

'It's cold upstairs. Get Agnes to find you some hot water bottles!'

Agnes followed sedately behind. 'You're off then, Mr Fenton? Well, thank you again for your help with the chimney.'

Keith Fenton's 'Goodnight' to me was cool, but Sarah squeezed my hands. 'Do ring up if there's anything you need. Be seeing you soon!'

Agnes saw them out and then bolted the outer door. In the kitchen I wondered if I should wash up or if Agnes would see that as interference. As I hesitated she came stalking in.

'The fire in the drawing-room is burning up fine now,' she said.

'Thank you.' Meekly I did as she wanted, leaving the comfort and warmth of the old kitchen for the cold austerities of the formal room. I wandered about, looking at the miscellany of pictures on the walls, examining the books in the glass-fronted cases. If only Sarah could have stayed! Or if Elinor could have been here! I felt so alone. There were framed photographs on the grand piano and I looked at them with interest. I recognised my grandparents. There were several pictures of my father as a boy and as a young man. There was no wedding photograph, no photograph of my mother. There was one of a little girl and I realised with a shock that I was the child.

I flopped down on the rug beside the fire. The logs had burned fast, with a fierce heat. I watched a glowing cavern crumble. I had been a fool to come. I could never live here. The practical difficulties were too immense. Next day I would go through my grandparents' things, mark on the inventory any items I would like to buy back from the estate once the valuation was completed. It would go for auction, Briarybank, and Keith Fenton would buy it, for he wanted it. He would have to pay a stiff price for it if the spec builder was after it, but that would not be my concern, or—because of death duties—my gain. He would have the Dower House to dump his mother and sister in when his father was off exploring and he wanted to bring a bride to Fenton House.

There was a tap on the door and Agnes Bruce came in. She stood in that sedate way of hers, with her hands folded together.

'Will there be anything else, Miss Lorimer?'

'Oh no, thank you. Nothing more.'

'Your room is first on the right when you go up the stairs. The bathroom is next door to it. Would you be wanting breakfast before nine?'

It was on the tip of my tongue to say I'd see to my own breakfast, but that would lead only to more fuss. She would have to fetch food over from her own cottage now, and she was obviously and understandably wanting to be clear.

'Nine o'clock will do very nicely,' I said. I attempted a smile but her face muscles didn't move. She nodded almost imperceptibly. 'Very well,' she said, 'goodnight.'

I put another log on the fire, remembering what Sarah had said, and sat close to the hearth to get the full benefit of the blaze. Then I raked back the ashes and put out the light. As I mounted the broad stairs I realised that now I was quite alone in the house. The old boards creaked. Rising wind threshed the trees outside. I had watched too many horror movies not to feel a frisson of unease. I glanced at the paintings as I went up past them. The landscapes were dark and gloomy but innocuous. It was the portraits that unnerved me. Eyes seemed to fix on me, move as I moved. Had they frightened me when I was here as a child? I had no conscious memory, but

45

the mind plays strange tricks. If the portraits
had been a terror I could well have forgotten
them. And then I came to the head of the stairs
and the last portrait and I stood transfixed. Not
in terror, but amazement. For he was here, my
knight. It was here I had seen that face, passing
it every day for weeks, coming to love it,
standing by it for hours and dreaming—for I
remembered now. And how like he was! I stood
and took in every detail—the dark background
with its hint of forest, the strong features, the
fine eyes, the nobility of expression, the stern
line of helmet and armour, the elegance of wrist
that held the falcon. I peered at old letters at the
bottom of the painting. There was a name,
D'Artois, Dubois—I couldn't be certain. Not
Fenton. And yet it might have been a portrait of
Keith Fenton. Or could it? The bone structure
here was altogether more delicate. My knight
was idealised, all romance. Keith Fenton was
robust. He had his feet on the ground and he
would be able to laugh at himself. As a man he
would be rather wonderful to know. A pang
caught me totally unawares and I leant
trembling against the banisters. Then I forced
myself forward along the corridor and into the
Yellow Room. The chill took my breath away. I
would have been more comfortable in
Bideawee. And altogether very much happier in
the Manchester flat with Elinor to talk to and
Justin dropping in. Here I was finding

heartache—heartache over grandparents I had scarcely known, heartache over a house that I had thought might be home, heartache over a romantic dream that was fusing with knowledge of a real man.

And then, folding down the sheets, I found that an electric blanket had been switched on. Which, somehow, in a homely and in a heady way, was reassuring.

*　　*　　*

I awoke to rain, running down the windows, filling the gutters, washing the last golden leaves off the cherry tree outside my window. I could see why Sarah coveted the Yellow Room. In spite of its ugly wallpaper and the heavy furniture, it could have been in a tree house. Lying in bed I could almost feel the lift and fall of the cherry branches tossed in the wind. A side window looked over the wood to my Shining Hill. Only today my hill was a shadow in the grey sheets of rain.

At nine o'clock punctually I presented myself in the kitchen. Agnes, an apron over a neat coat and skirt, served me the kind of breakfast I could have expected in a good hotel.

'There was no need to go to such trouble,' I said, 'especially on Sunday morning. Tea and a slice of toast—'

Her mouth remained tight and I said no

more. Clearing away, she said, 'I've lit the fire in the drawing-room. If you wanted to use the study there's an electric fire.'

I wandered into the drawing-room. With the curtains open and the rain streaming on the laurels outside, it was bleak and cheerless. The study, being smaller, might be easier to warm up. I switched on the fire, both bars, dismissing a feeling of guilt. I would be paying the electricity bill, after all. The study had a look of having been lived in. Two large shiny leather chairs faced each other across the hearth. Here the book shelves were open and many of the books paper-back. I studied the titles and gradually discerned two distinct strands of taste. Someone had been passionately fond of historical novels and biography. Someone had been a detective story addict. There was a massive desk, its top of fine green leather, with elaborate antique ink-stands in silver. An assortment of odds and ends cluttered the mantelpiece and window ledges, some quaint wood carvings, a Greek vase, badly chipped but surely not genuine? Victorian musical boxes and exotic shells.

I had taken up an ivory fan when the door behind me opened suddenly and I jumped, setting the fan down in a hurry as though I had been caught going through a stranger's cupboards. It was old Jessie Bruce. She wore a woollen shawl over a thick tweed dress, her feet

48

in wellington boots.

I smiled my relief. 'Good morning!'

'I widna call it that,' she said in her downright way. 'Is she lookin' after ye?'

'Agnes? Why, yes.'

'She's awa' to the kirk.'

'In this rain?'

'Aye.' Jessie looked at one of the leather chairs and then up at me. 'She gets the bus at the gate here.'

'Do sit down!'

She did so and put her hands out to the electric fire. The veins stood out, there was only skin between the finger bones.

'Ye havena brought your man?'

My 'wee bit mannie'! I repressed the urge to giggle.

'Not this time.'

'And you are a teacher, they tell me? In Manchester.'

'Yes.'

'I've never been south o' the Border. I've had nae wish to wander far frae Briarybank.'

And now she might have to leave her little house.

I said, 'I can understand that.'

She looked at me, all sharpness, like a pantomime witch.

'I doot it, my lass.' She shook her head and sighed. 'Your grandfaither could ha' been content wi' Briarybank and nothing else. And

49

your faither, puir laddie—Aye, but that mother o' yours!'

I was coming up against old resentments and old prejudice and I didn't want that.

'I remember my father so well,' I said. 'He used to tell me stories.'

'About the Border reivers.'

'Reivers?'

'Scots and English baith, along the Marches, stealing each other's cattle.'

'He knew the sad old songs and the ballads—' I sank down in the second leather chair.

'"And seest thou there that bonnie road
That winds aboot the fernie brae?
That is the road to fair Elfland
Where thou and I maun gang this day."'

The old woman looked at me with eyes that had moistened.

'I can see him in ye, the puir laddie. He didna deserve what he got!'

I hadn't realised I had known the ballad. It had come flooding back to me, as other things were coming back. I remembered my father as reserved and sad and old. And yet he couldn't have been much over thirty when he died.

'I've heard them say, your grandparents, that he had na the will to live.' She shook her head. 'But they were bitter. I couldna go along wi' them there.'

'Why on earth should they say that?'

50

She gave me a long considering look. Then she drew herself up briskly. 'That's a' in the past, Miss Lucy. It doesna do to dwell on the past.'

'But I want to know, Mrs Bruce. Why should anyone think that about my father?'

My mother might not have fulfilled all his needs. There must have been areas of his mind where they never met. But that isn't enough for a young man with a family and congenial work to seek out his end under a London bus.

'If your mother didna tell you, it's no' for me to tell you!'

But my mother had never known, whatever it was that old Jessie Bruce was reluctant to tell me. It came back, the telephone conversation I had had with my mother at the beginning of the week.

'There was someone else he really wanted to marry, wasn't there? She went off with someone else. And he settled for my mother as a kind of second-best. Is that it?'

'Aye.' Jessie Bruce heaved a great sigh and strength seemed to ebb from her. 'Aye,' she said, 'that's aboot right.'

'Who was it he really loved?'

'Auld history,' she whispered. 'Auld history that's best forgotten.'

I got up and went into the kitchen with some idea of making coffee. It was cold. Old Jessie was frail. Talking with me about the past had

51

upset her. It disturbed me too. I wanted the facts about my father and my mother and the bitterness that had soured the last years of my grandparents' life. I had a right to know, so that I could understand. I didn't want to take advantage of an old family servant. I doubted if the lawyer would be able to tell me what I needed to know. I hunted in the kitchen cupboards. There was no coffee that I could see, only a tea caddy. As I turned towards the kettle I caught sight of a bottle. It was half-full of port wine. Used as a quick pick-me-up by the taciturn Agnes? I found two small tumblers and splashed some wine in each.

'Here you are!' Back in the study I handed a glass to old Jessie Bruce. 'To keep the cold out!'

She sipped appreciatively and sucked in her shrunken lips.

'That's grand!' she said. 'Left over from the funeral. Winna have a drop o' anything in oor ain hoose, will Agnes! Och, I dinna hold wi' that!'

She enjoyed her port unashamedly, grinning at me conspiratorially.

'I'll hae to suck a peppermint afore she comes back!'

I hadn't deliberately set out to loosen Jessie's tongue but the wine succeeded where tea might not have helped. She rambled on for a bit about my grandfather. What she said, added to memory and to what my mother had told me, built up a picture of a forceful old man with a romantic passionate nature. My grandmother remained shadowy. I had an impression of someone quiet and gentle, but whether she was negative and under the thumb of my colourful grandfather or whether she had steel under the velvet and was the tougher of the two I couldn't tell.

'I mind so weel the summer they came to Briarybank! Wee John—your faither—would be two years old. My Agnes was fourteen and was going into service with Mrs Edward Fenton. She was expectin' her second, that was Miss Marianne—'

'Marianne?'

'Aye, Marianne, the cause o' a' the trouble.'

I felt a shock of surprise. Marianne Fenton and my father?

'This Marianne—' I wrestled with relationships.

Old Jessie said briskly, 'The Colonel's sister. Mr Keith's aunt.'

'Where is she now?'

'Where she went, the limmer! In France. Madame Soora, they call her now. And little guid it did her! She might as weel ha' stayed at hame and married your faither like everybody expected. But your puir faither—a fine lad he was then, an' a'—was studying at the art college doon in London and brought hame this braw Frenchie and there was nae mair sense in her

53

heid. Oh, he pleaded wi' her—your faither, I mean—for he worshipped the ground she walked on. They a' pleaded wi' her. But she widna listen to reason. In the end auld Fenton gave in. He aye had a soft spot for his lassie and I daresay you couldna blame him either, for she was as bonny as the Flower o' Yarrow. He gave her a fine wedding. I mind your grand-faither—'*Fenton!*' I wasna listenin' at ony door. The two o' them were in this very room and you could hear them through the hoose—'*Fenton, your daughter is promised to my son. If you give her away to that French paint-dauber I'll never speak to you again!*' And he didna. Never a word. The two o' them that had been sich friends. From that minute on, the guid times were over at Briarybank.'

The feud! So this was how it had been!

'Your faither stayed awa' in London. They wanted him hame but he widna come. I mind the day they got the news he was going to get married. Och, your grandfather was a terrible man! He ranted and raved. I thocht he would hae a seizure. Your grandmother calmed him doon. But he widna go the wedding in London and your grandmother widna go withoot him. They sat in here. She grat, the puir soul, and he said nothing. Nothing for days. And then your faither brought hame his bride.'

Old Jessie hitched her shawl on her shoulders. I found my hands were tight-clasped

54

in my lap. My poor mother! What chance had she had? It would have taken a very exceptional young woman to cope successfully with that situation.

Jessie was watching me with her faded blue eyes.

'I was sorry for that lass. She was a bonnie bit thing, wi' a nice wee waist and a wide skirt and dainty high-heeled shoes. Oh, nane o' your jeans i' thae days! But she was cowed, the puir cratur. She was feert o' your faither. Oh, the change in him! He had gaen awa' a laddie and come back a man. And she was mair feert o' your grandfaither. Your grandmother tried to be kind, but your puir mother didna ken how to behave—'

'What do you mean?'

'Weel, she chattered when she'd ha' been better to have held her tongue! If she wasna like a rabbit fixed by a weasel, she blethered. She blethered to me, she blethered awa' to Agnes. Oh, Agnes had been back here long before the trouble came. I couldna ha' managed this place on my ain.

'Of course your grandfaither had had the right o' it. *"Withhold her portion!"* I can hear him yet, thunderin' awa' at auld Fenton. "Cut off her money and see what happens then! I'm willing to wager my ten acres that her precious Frenchman will slink away!"'

Jessie had an instinct for the dramatic. Those

55

could well have been my grandfather's very words.

'But auld Fenton was aye a proud devil. He wasna to be dictated to by an Edinburgh lawyer! "I daresay", says he, "the French paint-dauber's pedigree is as long as yours, Lorimer!" That finished it. Though he would never have admitted it, Robert Lorimer would ha' given his right hand to belong to the gentry. It wasna for Marianne's looks and brains that he was set on his son marryin' her. And it wasna for her money. It was so that his grandchildren wid be gentry!'

I sat back limply in the old leather chair. The pain of it all—my grandfather's aspirations, his bitter disappointment, his absurd pride. New ideas had overtaken his world. What had once mattered to a romantic steeped in Scottish history was out-of-date, meaningless, empty.

'The Fentons,' I said in a deepening resentment that I should have seen as irrational, 'do they have such a marvellous pedigree?'

Old Jessie was tiring. A keenness that had brightened in her eyes had ebbed away. 'Oh aye. They can trace the line back unbroken to the time o' Robert the Bruce.'

The portrait upstairs and the likeness continuing!

'Not that they were Fentons then. It was Dartie. The descent comes through the female line. The first o' them cam' ower frae

56

Normandy wi' the Conqueror—'

I gave a scornful snort. 'So they're French too!'

Jessie looked at me uncomprehendingly. Her knowledge of history had its limitations and was not supported by any understanding of geography.

'They had land in England at one time, but they lost it after the Rebellion.' Irritation sparked in her face. 'The Rebellion in 1745 when Bonnie Prince Charlie—'

I smiled. 'I *do* know! Even though my mother is English and I was brought up in London!'

'Aye, weel, you did say your faither told you the auld stories!' She levered herself to her feet. 'I'll have to be gettin' back. Agnes widna like to ken that we've been havin' this wee bit crack!'

'That's all right, Mrs Bruce. I won't mention it.' I glanced up at the window. 'The rain's still coming down. I'll get a brolly and walk back with you.'

I fetched an umbrella and armed her through the kitchen. 'The old feud seems to be over now. Agnes said Mr Fenton had seen to things for my grandparents.'

'Oh, there was no feud as far as Mr Keith was concerned. When the auld laird died Mr Keith took over Fenton, for the Colonel never took the least bit o' interest in the place. Spends a' his time i' the army, awa' foreign. And he kind o' took the place o' the son they had lost. In truth, I expected they'd leave him Briarybank!'

We paused at the back door. I hadn't looked for this!

'Did *he* expect it?'

'It must ha' crossed his mind. It's my ain belief they meant to, but never got the will changed. They kent weel enough that he wants the place.'

I elbowed her over to her own front door. I should have liked to be sure her fire was burning, but she didn't ask me in. I walked back across the courtyard in the chilling rain.

Since Agnes had taken the trouble to light the drawing-room fire I replenished it and settled there although I should have preferred the study. I made no attempt to explore the house. I simply knelt on the rug with the mass of my new knowledge.

I had lost all sense of time and it was with surprise that I saw a bus draw up on the road and Agnes come hurrying up the drive. As the grandfather clock in the hall struck one, she came into the drawing-room with a tray and set my lunch out on a side table. I longed to say, 'Cut the formality! I'd rather eat in the kitchen.' I wished she would pass over a few tins from her cottage and let me fend for myself. But her standards were inflexible. I was Miss Lorimer of Briarybank and would receive the first-class service to which she thought I was entitled, while at the same time she made me feel an opportunist and the interloper I was.

When she came to clear away she brought me a bunch of keys. She indicated the keys for the outer doors, the keys of certain cupboards and chests, the keys of the desk. I wasn't sure that I had the right to take them.

'I have copies of the house door keys,' she said and left me.

I sat on in the drawing-room, watching the rain streaming down the window panes. I had no wish to use the keys Agnes had given me. Originally I had planned to look at the house objectively with the idea I had had for setting up a school, but this afternoon I felt the idea too absurd to harbour with any seriousness. There was no place for me here, in spite of the feelings I had had the week before in the woods. My future was not in Briarybank—only strands of the past that had been overlaid and, very soon, would be overlaid again, for good. The house should have gone to Keith Fenton, who loved it and wanted it and, in human terms, had a right to it. I had no right. It was small wonder he resented my coming. Then something struck me with such force that I was physically winded. Was it possible that my grandparents could have made a new will? Without consulting the Edinburgh lawyer? Or any lawyer? Wouldn't a dated, witnessed document be legally valid, even if no lawyer had drawn it up? Perhaps, after all, I should make a search of the desk.

The telephone ringing jolted me into silly panic. Who could be calling? Elinor? I took up the receiver.

A woman's voice that I hadn't heard before spoke in my ear.

'Miss Lorimer? How do you do? I'm Margaret Fenton. You've met my son Keith and my Sarah. I gather you're on your own at Briarybank. What a ghastly day, isn't it?'

Taken completely by surprise, I missed what she said next. Then stupidly I realised she was asking me over to Fenton House for dinner.

'Do come! It will be so nice to meet you. Don't expect anything grand! We usually eat off trays in front of the telly. Keith will pick you up. About seven?'

I slumped back on the rug, wishing I had had the presence of mind to produce an excuse. The last thing I wanted was to meet more Fentons! She sounded thoroughly nice, though, this mother of Keith and Sarah. And Sarah had been fun. But somehow, although the feud was long over, they were the enemy. I must let Agnes know in good time that I wouldn't be needing an evening meal. It was on my way back from the Bruces' cottage that I realised the rain had stopped. The cloud was lifting quickly and in the west there were streaks of reddish colour. The telephone call, Mrs Fenton's pleasant voice and kind words, had cut across the over-heated emotional lather into which I had lashed myself. I wanted not to slip back into it. The idea of another will was far-fetched. Someone, surely, would have checked.

I took a brisk walk, along the road for I hadn't footwear suitable for the sodden woods. The late afternoon felt balmy. It was as though the rain had taken the cold sting from the air. I put everything out of my mind, old Jessie's stories of the past, the problems of the present, and enjoyed the physical exercise, the peace, the great swelling lines of the hills. Hedgerow sounds drew me. I saw birds I couldn't put a name to, I watched young rabbits scampering to the safety of their holes. I hadn't been beyond Briarybank before. The road crested the shoulder of what was my Shining Hill, dipped gently and I found myself passing very splendid gates in metalwork of elaborate design. They were open to a drive that swept up an avenue of trees. What lay beyond was hidden from the road by a fold in the land, but I could guess it was Fenton House.

At this point I turned back. It was going to be dark early. It could possibly rain again soon. Seeing the Fenton gates punctured my peace of mind. If he had so much, a great mansion in a fine estate, why did Keith Fenton covet my little house? What would possessing it do for him, beyond restoring what had once been an entity, clearing up what he could only see as an untidiness? His grandfather had sold the house to my grandfather. My father would have inherited the house if he had lived. My father had died—an unhappy man because of Fenton fickleness. I owed Fenton nothing beyond the courtesy of a neighbour. The emotions of the afternoon I saw now as absurd. I crested the shoulder of my hill and saw the house. It gleamed white among the darkening trees. A light shone dimly from the hall. Smoke went straight up from two chimneys. I stopped. Aloud, I said,

'Briarybank, *my* house!'

It was warm and shabbily welcoming when I stepped into the hall. I drew the drawing-room curtains, made tea in the kitchen and carried it through to my seat on the hearth. How suddenly a mood can swing! I couldn't finish my tea quickly enough to start out on a tour of inspection of a house that might be turned into a school!

Nothing, I told myself, was impossible. The study I would keep more or less as it was, for my own use. The drawing-room and the dining-room would form the class-rooms. The rooms in the keep could be developed in all sorts of exciting ways. The kitchen premises would have to be gutted and entirely re-formed and modernised. There was room and to spare to provide cloakrooms and toilet facilities. The garden at the back was enclosed and could be made safe for children playing. I went upstairs. The principal bedroom above the drawing-room I could have as a sitting-room. There were bedrooms for Elinor and for me and two over. Elinor could have her own sitting-room if she wanted. This all rather depended on Elinor coming in with me! But if Elinor wouldn't, then someone else would. Or I might find someone local who would live at home. But would it pay, I wondered. There would have to be serious sessions with paper and calculator. I was assuming there would be a demand for nursery school places in Clerkstoun. For all I knew Clerkstoun might have more nursery schools than it could fill. I should have to do a bit of research, asking around, and with care and tact.

I walked along the landing, my heart hammering with excitement. It was not impossible. I could sell some of the antiques to cover the cost of alterations and decoration. I started down the staircase and I saw him, my knight. I stopped. A finer, romantic Keith! And suddenly I realised the time and remembered that the real, flesh-and-blood Keith was picking me up in half an hour!

I had not brought much with me in the way of clothes, not having anticipated dinner invitations. From the wardrobe I took out the only possible, a dress of soft blue wool, with a gold chain for belt. I had trouble with my hair

63

from my walk in the damp evening and was still in my room when I heard a car engine on the drive. It was dark now and from the window I could see nothing but the beam of headlights. The door bell rang and rang again as I fumbled into shoes and snatched a coat. I heard Agnes go to the door, her voice and Keith's. I ran downstairs. They were waiting in the hall. He was wearing light slacks and a dark roll-top sweater. His chestnut hair was well-brushed and touched with a shining mist of moisture. He was half-smiling in the easy way he had, one corner of his mouth lifting towards the deep cleft in his cheek.

'It's drizzling,' he said. 'Be ready for a quick dive to the car.'

Agnes said, 'There was a telephone call for you, Miss Lorimer, not long after you were over at the cottage. I looked in all the rooms.'

'That must have been when I was out.'

'You had not mentioned that you would be going out.'

'I went on the spur of the moment—when I saw the rain had stopped. Was there a message?'

'Mr Justin Wain said he would ring again. I took the liberty of telling him you were going out for the evening and so he said he would make it half-past ten.'

So Justin had tracked me down!

'Thank you,' I said crisply. If my annoyance

came through so much the better! She could have let me know there had been a phone call. If she had not wanted to come over to the house she could have left a note. I could have rung Justin. He would be vexed with me for having dashed off north, after allowing him and Elinor to believe that I was going to my mother in London. He was a good friend. He did not deserve such cavalier treatment. My conscience had been pricking me. With Keith Fenton waiting there was nothing I could do for now.

He hurried me over the drive and into a car. No Landrover tonight!

'It's very kind of your mother to ask me,' I said. 'I feel rather bad butting into your Sunday evening.'

He put the car round in a tight lock that sent me jolting against him. 'Sorry about that! The drive could do with a bit of widening. There's no butting in, I do assure you. The girls are wild for a bit of company. You took a trick with Sarah.'

Already we were on the steep stretch of road I had trudged that afternoon. 'She's fun!'

Keith Fenton gave a brotherly snort.

'I gather she gave you a highly-coloured account of my father's life-style?'

'She told me he is an explorer.'

'He goes on army expeditions to uncomfortable places, which you might say is the same thing. When he is away Mother goes

65

south on a round of family visits. She has three sisters and a brother, each with a family and they adore her. Departure date has been delayed and she's chafing.'

There could be no great need for him to acquire what had been the Dower House. Would his parents ever want to rusticate at Briarybank?

He turned in at the splendid wrought-iron gates. The tree-lined drive was long, swinging on a wide curve round enclosed shrubberies and gardens. The night was dark and I could see practically nothing. He drew up at what I learned later was a side entrance and led me into a conservatory. Here warmth and plant fragrance touched me like mink. The lighting was low. I glimpsed a luxuriance of ferns and ivies, the occasional splash of exotic flower colour. A nymph drooped sightlessly over a wide stone basin and poured trickling water from a stone jar. He pushed open a door and stood aside to let me pass into a hall. It was what I had expected—vast, marble-floored, with sculptured columns picked out in blue and gold. Against the walls handsome Victorian pieces that, singly, would have dwarfed the hall in Briarybank, seemed slight and insignificant. Here and there were tiny-seeming rugs that would have fitted my drawing-room. The staircase that swept upwards was in keeping with the entrance, broad, marble, elegant.

He opened a door to a cloakroom where I left my coat. Then with clattering heels I followed him across the marble. By a door towards the back of the entrance hall he paused, glancing at me, smiling.

'Relax!'

Resenting him for seeing too much I flared up and he opened the door. 'Hello, everyone!' he called. 'May I introduce Miss Lorimer of Briarybank!'

The spurt of annoyance he had called up carried me over the worst moment of facing a roomful of strangers. Or so it seemed then. I was conscious of many lamps, a leaping fire, soft carpeting and chintzy chairs, dogs and people. Somehow I hadn't expected the dogs. But they moved beautifully, like the people. Keith's mother was beside me in the instant, taking my hands, drawing me into the room. She wore her greying hair in a short chunky style. She had fine bone-structure and a good skin. I suspected she wore no make-up. In dark slacks and a loose silk top she gave an impression of being slim.

'My dear, this is so good of you!' In that low-pitched voice she spoke as though I were conferring a favour. 'Sarah you already know—'

In a pretty dress with her hair brushed out, Sarah grinned and said, 'Hi!'

'My husband, Colonel Fenton—'

Keith's father resembled him and yet I

67

sensed the two men totally unlike. He was tall, well-built. The military training showed. His skin was coarsened from weather and permanently tanned. His hair, shorter than his son's, was only lightly touched with grey and just as thick. He had a ready grin, like Sarah's. He took my hand in a grip that pinched.

'Welcome to Fenton!' he said. 'There's nothing we can do about the weather, I'm afraid. What will you have to drink?'

I murmured something about sherry and turned to the remaining stranger. She was of medium height, elegantly slender and quite startlingly beautiful. Her most striking feature was her forehead, broad and high, from which soft brown hair rose in a kind of aureole. Her eyebrows were exquisitely drawn, her large blue eyes enhanced by just the right amount of make-up. Her lipstick was a brilliant red against the honey colour of her skin.

Mrs Fenton spoke and I heard the name Estelle, but I made out no more as Colonel Fenton cut across with 'Medium or dry?'

'Maybe,' said Sarah, 'Lucy would prefer sweet!'

'Only little girls like sweet,' said Keith.

I looked from Mrs Fenton to the Colonel and laughed. 'I would actually prefer sweet!'

They all laughed with me and we settled into chairs. Except Sarah who sprawled on the rug between the golden retrievers.

'You haven't introduced me to them,' I said.

Sarah lifted up one drowsy paw and then another. 'Rose and Cavalier,' she said.

Estelle arched her brows and Keith said, 'Oh dear!'

Colonel Fenton handed me a glass, murmuring, 'Sweets to the sweet!' and Keith said, 'Oh dear!' again.

By the time we went into the small room that the family were using as a dining-room I felt we had all been friends for a long time.

Conversation never flagged for an instant. Estelle laid herself out to be pleasant to me, asking about my job, the training I had had. She knew London well and found it hard to understand my leaving it from choice. The talk moved to foreign places. I longed to hear something of Colonel Fenton's travels but Estelle, finding I had been to the Dalmatian coast, stayed with that. She discovered I had holidayed in Korcula. She knew the island and we experienced the pleasure people have when they find they have eaten in the same restaurants, wandered the same narrow streets.

'It's so romantic,' she murmured in her husky voice that sometimes held the echo of a foreign accent. 'Especially in the moonlight, when the old people and the children have gone to bed, and left the world to—'

'Estelle,' said Mrs Fenton, 'do you think we should have coffee here or in the sitting-room?'

Estelle elected to have coffee in the sitting-room. 'I'll get it,' she said, rising slinkily and ruffling Keith's hair as she passed behind his chair, 'if Keith will come and help me.'

Colonel Fenton led me back to the fire. He threw on more logs and sparks went up the wide chimney in showers. I was conscious of an argument going on behind me between Sarah and her mother, and when Sarah came back to her place on the hearth-rug there was high colour in her cheeks and she looked sulky.

Coffee was a long time in coming. Now I was able to ask Colonel Fenton about his forthcoming expedition, but my mind was not wholly on what he told me about the journey he would be undertaking in the next few months in the Sahara. Who was Estelle? Something tugged at my memory. Was she in love with Keith, and he with her? With neither of them would it be easy to tell. Sarah was bothered about something. Was it that she didn't like Estelle and didn't want her beloved brother to marry her?

When the coffee arrived Estelle handed it with liqueurs. I had had wine with dinner. The heat of the fire combined with the drinks to make me relaxed and drowsy. Conversation meandered pleasantly on. Colonel Fenton launched out on stories of his adventures, stories that the others must have heard before. He was an enthralling story-teller and I felt in a rarefied mood, on a different plane of living from the everyday. I was vexed when Keith interrupted and said,

'If you are to get back in time for that phone call—'

Justin! I had completely forgotten.

Keith did his best to extricate me, but no one seemed any keener for the evening to end than I was. I had my coat on and we were standing in the hall, discussing a possible get-together later in the week, and whether Sarah might ride over to Briarybank in the morning.

Mrs Fenton said, 'What a pity you aren't staying on in Briarybank!'

'Have you fixed a date for the sale?' asked Colonel Fenton.

I looked round at my new friends and said happily,

'I'm not selling.'

There was a silence that seemed to go on in that large cold marble hall. Then everybody spoke at once.

'*Really*? I understood it was settled?' The Colonel was puzzled.

Sarah, drawn two ways, said, 'But I thought that *we*—' and then '—so you will be our *neighbour*!'

Estelle, her lovely face radiating a pleasure I had not expected, cried, 'Why, Lucy, that's wonderful news! We may call you Lucy, mayn't we? Especially now!'

Mrs Fenton said, 'But how could you live in that old place, a young girl like you?'

Only Keith said nothing. I had seen his face the moment I spoke. He had turned pale, his mouth drawing to a taut line and his eyes sparking with fierce protest.

CHAPTER THREE

It was Keith who got me away from the mounting questions.

'Lucy is expecting a trunk call at half-past ten!' he said firmly. 'She will fix a press-conference in due course. Meantime, "No comment!"'

I was still calling my thanks for a lovely evening when he plunged me into the dimness of the conservatory. In the car he put his foot down hard.

'This is very good of you,' I said. 'I do appreciate it. But if Justin rings before I'm home I can ring him back.'

'No doubt,' he said drily. 'But you don't want to be too rough on him.'

We went very fast down the drive. There must have been pot-holes for we had some hard bumps. We swept out at the ornate gates.

'Aren't you interested that I'm not selling Briarybank?'

He said, 'It's none of my business.'

'I'd heard you were interested.'

'Sarah? She gets fancies.'

'Not only Sarah. It's common talk.'

'You will find that staying in a small community one is always the subject of talk, one way or another.'

He was determined not to show that he cared about the house. Did he suspect me of playing games, trying to push up the price? Or had he taken a knock he wasn't yet ready to face? He got me to the front door of Briarybank two minutes short of half-past ten, and as he prepared to drive off he heard the telephone start to ring.

Breathless, caught in the magic of the evening, and an awareness of other things, I would have given much not to have had to speak to Justin then.

There were no preambles. 'What the hell do you think you're up to?'

'I beg your pardon?'

'You told me you were going down to London for mid-term.'

'I told you no such thing!'

'Told me in so many words, maybe not! But you let me think it. And Elinor too.'

'I don't have to account to you for what I do!'

I was being cheap and I knew it.

'You don't have to, no! But one expects a degree of trust between friends. I thought we were friends. Like a bloody fool I believed we were more than friends—'

'Justin—'

'When I rang and got Elinor and heard you'd already left I was so sure you'd have left a note for me that I went round. Only there was no note, and there I was looking a proper Charley with your friend Elinor smiling under her lashes. I spoke to your mother then. She didn't even know it was your mid-term. And after that I realised it could only be your precious Briarybank.'

'I was going to ring you, Justin. Honestly.'

'Were you? When? And I gather from that hatchet-faced retainer of yours that you've been out hob-nobbing with your landed neighbours—'

'I'm sure that Agnes with all her shortcomings would not say what I was doing.'

'Trained to be discreet, is she? "Miss Lorimer has a dinner engagement this evening"!' Justin mimicked Agnes' stiff strongly-accented words. 'Was it *à deux* with that stiff-necked aristo—'

'Justin! The Fentons very kindly asked me over.'

'All right, all right! But Lucy Lorimer, what *are* you up to?'

'Oh, Justin, I don't know! I think I want to keep this house!'

'But you can't!'

'Maybe I could.'

'It's not on, poppet. Okay, it's a fine old place and it belonged to your grandparents and you remember being there when you were little, but it's a hard world. What would you live on? Who would you have for company, apart from Hatchet and the Aristo? You'd get bored crazy in a matter of weeks. Look, darling, don't think I don't understand! But be sensible! We're snowed under at the Institute this week. I can't get away before Friday—'

'—but—'

'Friday I can wangle. I'll be up with you by mid-day, right? Don't do anything irrevocable before then, will you?'

I chewed my lip as I clutched the phone.

'Promise me?'

'Things move so slowly in this kind of business that I'm not likely to do anything irrevocable for quite some time.'

'We've got to talk, Lucy Lorimer. Properly talk. But not on the phone. You with me?'

I was with him all right.

'So until Friday,' he said.

I found it difficult to get to sleep that night. My thoughts turned in a relentless roundabout. One minute Justin was right, I was indulging a crazy dream; the next I was wholly committed to living on in this place I already loved. I saw the echoing splendours of Fenton House and the contrasting warmth of the family scene. I saw the faces of Sarah and her father, of Mrs Fenton and Estelle. Only Keith I shied from. His image fused with the picture of my knight and disturbed me. My knight was serene but Keith was angry. Keith resented my coming here and my staying.

Next morning I slept late and tumbled downstairs to find Agnes waiting breakfast for me in the study.

'I thought it would be more comfortable for you here,' she said. I understood she wanted her kitchen to herself.

It was a glorious morning. There had been a hard frost and outside every tree, every shrub, every late-lingering leaf was crusted with brilliant crystals. The sky was a clear hard blue. Behind the frosted wood my hill was shining. This was just how I remembered it! I could hardly wait to be out of doors. Crossing the stream was no problem. The ground on either side was frozen hard and only the fast-moving mainstream of water was free of ice. I went through the gate and up the hill. The freshness of the air caught my throat. The stillness was deep. Sheep crunched on the frozen grass, rooks squabbled excitably in a knot of trees. From the crest of my Shining Hill the view was superb. The Border hills fell away on all sides, fold after fold. Clerkstoun, beautified by frost and distance, lay in the valley like a dream place. In the other direction Fenton House was hidden under the swelling flank of the hill. I looked about me for the Standing Stones. There had been two tall stones, I remembered, one of them bound by a rusting iron bar. My grandfather had told me how they had been placed there by the ancient people, how they were old when Wallace and Bruce were leading the Scottish armies in battle with the English. I had wanted him to climb the Shining Hill with me so that we could see the Stones together, but he had been too busy. I realised now that he would have felt unable to put foot on Fenton land, although it could be overlooked in a child. I scrambled round an outcrop of rock, fought my way through a thicket of whins. And then I saw them. The stone that had been supported by the iron band had collapsed. The other, half-lost in whins, was no higher than I was. What had been vast and mysterious to the child I had been was small-scale and subject to natural disintegration. Through a blurring of romantically self-indulgent emotion, I saw two figures on horse-back come into view under the flank of the hill. One was Keith. I knew that instantly. Was the other Sarah? Sarah had said she might ride over that morning. It wouldn't do for me to be out when she arrived. From the way the riders were heading they could be making for Briarybank. My emotion over the symbol of the shrunken stone forgotten, I turned and hurtled down the hillside. I startled a hare which fled leaping from me. I narrowly missed falling over a sheltering sheep. Glowing from the exertion I burst into the kitchen. I was only too ready to make coffee myself but Agnes left vegetables she was preparing and took up the percolator.

'I will bring it in when you ring,' she said. 'You will be in the study?'

I dashed upstairs to comb out my hair and put on some lipstick. I avoided looking at my knight as I passed him on my way down. They would come in at the back, I reckoned, and so I posted myself at the window. It would not do to appear too eager, and so, with the need to write to Elinor in mind, I took up a writing-pad. But the minutes ticked past. No one came. There was no sound of horses' hooves on the cobbled yard. I looked at the clock. It was well after half-past eleven. The coffee would be stewed. Should I ring for a cup or wait? Absurdly disappointed I sat on by the window. 'My dear Elinor,' I had written. What was I going to say? *I am sitting here at the study window looking up at the Shining Hill, waiting for him to come*. Because that was how it was. It was no use pretending. And I was a fool, a complete fool.

It was nearly mid-day when a clattering on the cobbles brought me trembling to my feet. I saw Sarah dismount and draw her horse into one of the abandoned stables. I rang the bell. Agnes was bringing in the coffee when Sarah

78

tapped on the study window.

She came in, tugging off her cap, her cheeks red from the cold. 'Coffee—*lovely*!' She flashed her generous smile at Agnes and got a twitch of the lips in response.

Agnes left the room and Sarah smacked her riding crop against her breeches. 'I'm so *cross*!' she said. 'I'm bursting with crossness!'

'Dear me!' I handed her a cup of coffee. 'Sugar?'

'Please.' Sarah flopped beside me on the rug. It occurred to me that apart from when we were having dinner I had never seen Sarah sit in a chair. 'Estelle took Parsifal.'

'Biscuit?'

'Thanks. My horse. Estelle hardly ever rides. She *must* have heard me say last night that I'd ride over here this morning, yet she insists she didn't. And she keeps saying she meant only to go out for an hour, but that Keith—'

'I must have seen them earlier,' I said. 'I went up the hill.'

'It's glorious out, isn't it? There I was gasping to get into it, hanging on waiting for Estelle! Oh, she's supposed to have Parsifal if she wants a mount, but let's face it, the big out-of-doors is not Estelle's scene!'

'What is her scene?'

'Paris.'

'*Paris?*'

'Well, wouldn't you agree she looks it? And

being half-French—'

'I thought there was ze trace of ze foreign accent.'

'But you knew about my Aunt Marianne?'

'Aunt Marianne? I'm sorry I'm not with you.' And then suddenly I was. 'You mean—Estelle's mother—'

'Is Daddy's sister. And she married a romantic French painter called Raoul Seurat. Who ditched her quite soon afterwards—'

My father's Marianne!

'But she's a tough nut, my Aunt Marianne. She wasn't going to come creeping home to hear everybody saying, "We told you so!" She got herself a little shop and built up a fashion business. Oh heavens, nothing big! And not on the boulevards! It's in a shady little side-street off a side-street on the outskirts! But *les Parisiennes* like their chic dresses, and Aunt Marianne manages a little jam on her crust. Estelle helps her. She's good on design. Knows a nice style and good fabric when she sees it.'

Estelle and Keith were cousins! That could account for a close bond. But cousins could be in love! My hand shook slightly as I lowered my cup.

'Would you think me an awful pig if I had another biscuit?' Sarah helped herself and settled more comfortably on the rug. 'You are very well-mannered, Lucy.'

'What *do* you mean?'

'Well, in your place I'd be asking if Estelle is after Keith! But of course, why should you care?'

My heart jolted in a sickening way and I thought, *Why indeed?* I forced a grin. I hadn't asked because I hadn't dared. Now I could. 'Well, is she?'

'Obviously!'

'And your brother?'

'Keith's like a sphinx. He annoys me so much I could shake him and shake him!'

'Because he doesn't wear his heart on his sleeve?'

Sarah twisted up her face in the effort to express her feelings. 'I don't know him somehow, anymore. We used to be real friends. He used to be the most super fun. But now—'

He was in love with someone against his will? Someone who maddened his senses, someone who couldn't or wouldn't fit in with his way of life?

'It's funny, really, Mummy likes Estelle. Dad does, of course, but what man wouldn't! But Mummy's a surefire judge of character and she's not putting on an act about it. Dad just laughs at me and says I don't know anything about it and that Keith will end up marrying Antonia Crawford.'

'And who,' I asked, 'is Antonia Crawford?'

Sarah scrambled to her feet. 'Crikey, is that the time? I really shall have to go. Parsifal will have to be rubbed down, you see, and if I'm late for meals Dad does his nut. Antonia? Her father is the biggest mill-owner in Clerkstoun. They're rolling in it. She's nice, actually. I wouldn't mind if Keith married her—she's super at tennis and she rides really well—'

One way and another Keith had it made! No wonder he was edgy, having such a choice to make!

I got up. 'It's been lovely seeing you, Sarah, but I mustn't keep you and make you late.'

'Gosh, no!' She was half-way to the door when she said, 'Can I have some sugar for Parsifal? There was a nice lumpy bit—'

I walked out with her, watched her expert dealing with what was all mystery to me. She mounted as I'd seen girls do on the telly and she trotted off, her Parsifal arching his mane, blowing white breath into the frosty air.

Agnes brought me lunch on a tray and when I'd eaten I took up the writing-pad.

'Dear Elinor,

I came up here under some kind of compulsion. Somehow I had to see the house again. I've had a good look at it with the idea of turning it into a school. It could be done. Sometimes I have thought I want to have a go. But on balance I have to admit you're right. And Justin too! He rang last night. He is coming up for me on Friday. Can you still maintain he is selfishly motivated? And so, my

82

dear—'

The phone rang. Agnes answered it before I got to the door. I heard the murmur of her voice. I went back to my letter. Then Agnes knocked and said, 'It's Mr Fenton on the telephone, Miss Lorimer.'

I have always been able to smile, if not to laugh, at my absurdities and so I was pretty much at ease when I went to answer him, my twentieth-century knight!

'I hope Sarah wasn't late for lunch?'

'If she was,' he said, 'it wasn't her fault. Or yours!' he hastened to add. 'I'm afraid I spoiled your morning. Estelle came with me on my rounds that shouldn't have kept me long, but we found a broken fence and by the time we had rounded up the strays—'

'Well, I'm sure Sarah would appreciate your explanation,' I said. 'We managed a chat.'

Remembering what we had chatted about I dried up.

'And I imagine she ate you out of biscuits? Which is really why I'm ringing.'

'Sorry?'

'I'm driving into Clerkstoun, leaving in a quarter of an hour. You're bound to have shopping to do. Agnes is sterling, bless her heart, but I doubt if she stocks your favourite brand of coffee? It's no fun lugging things on the bus so I suggest you accept this practical offer!'

I did, telling myself as I got ready that it was a sensible neighbourly act on his part and reminding myself that Estelle would almost certainly be with him. But she wasn't. He greeted me cheerfully, throwing open the car door for me without getting out. He was in riding breeches with a suède jacket incongruously on top. My heart gave an odd little jolt as I saw the line of his jaw and the fold in his cheek that deepened when he gave that wry half-smile of his.

I was almost short with him on the drive to Clerkstoun because I was angry with myself. I had been around with men better-looking than Keith Fenton, for heaven's sake! I was no teenager just out of a young ladies' school!

'You may not realise it,' he said, jerking his head towards the high hedge on our left, 'but the land over there is yours.'

'Oh.' I looked at him. 'Under turnip?'

He took his eyes momentarily off the road and cocked one eyebrow which deepened that fold in his cheek. Dear God, I thought, the sooner I get back to Manchester the better for my peace of mind!

'Is that—' I forced my mind to practical matters '—where a certain spec builder wants to put up executive housing?'

I saw his jaw set. 'I believe so.'

'What would you say if I told you I was considering selling him a few acres?'

His hands tightened on the wheel. 'It's none of my business what you do.'

'But it is! If I sold land to a builder he would have to get planning permission before he'd pay building land prices. And to get planning permission he'd have to get the agreement of property-owners round about.'

'You seem to have gone into it all very thoroughly,' he said drily.

'Actually I haven't. I just picked up a little from the lawyer. But you don't have to worry. Even if I made a packet from selling out to the builder I'd lose it all on death duties!'

'Well,' he said, 'that's the first time I've known anything good derive from death duties!'

He parked in the central square, that ugly grey space among stone shut-looking buildings. 'I'm afraid I don't find Clerkstoun an attractive town,' I told him.

He seemed genuinely surprised. 'You'll find there are good things, once you know it.'

We got out and he gave me some directions. 'All the best shops are in the High Street. Would an hour suit you?'

I enjoyed my little shopping expedition. Apart from tasty items for the larder I bought some wool and a knitting pattern. Elinor had a birthday soon. She loved sweaters and she didn't knit. It would be a positive occupation on my long solitary evenings. I bought picture postcards to send to Justin and Elinor and to the family in London. The postcards did less than justice to the scenery. The colours were muted, the hills undramatic.

From the High Street I wandered down a side lane and found myself beside a river. There were tiny icicles on the long grass on the bank, splinters of ice around the rocks at the edge of the water. An iron footbridge led over the river to the mills that ranged squat and ugly on the farther side. The sun was still shining but any warmth it might have had earlier had ebbed away. Chilled I turned and made my way back towards the square. It had been good to have this hour alone. I was able to sort myself out. It was inevitable that I should find Keith Fenton attractive. There was his amazing resemblance to the knight in a picture that had excited my childhood imagination. He was, as far as I could see, a thoroughly nice person. With his problems, no doubt, but he kept them to himself. The announcement of my intention to keep Briarybank had caught him off-balance. He had wanted to acquire the property and my staying on did not suit his book. Against that, he made it plain that what I did with my own was not his affair. His driving me into Clerkstoun was proof that he was ready to be friendly—although on reflection I felt the idea had probably come from his mother! I had to guard against being childish, resenting him one minute for slights imagined, believing myself in love with him the next! And I would have to decide, in a really adult way, what I was going to do about the house. The letter begun to Elinor on the down-swing of the see-saw could not be posted yet.

Coming out of the High Street into the square I saw him lounge over to his car and bend to unlock it. An old man stopped and spoke to him. I saw him straighten, saw his smile ready and quick. They talked for a few moments and I was conscious of warm affection for him and a kind of pride. Which was all right. Sisterly, that was how my feelings must be!

He took my packages and shopping bag and piled them on the back seat. 'Are you chafing to get back?' he asked. 'Or would you like me to show you some of the glories of Clerkstoun?'

'I'd love to have the scales taken from my eyes!'

'It's odd,' he said as we skirted the square, 'I see it as beautiful.'

'It's familiar. And you've seen it in all seasons, with the trees green and the flowers blooming in the centre there, and it all comes together for you.'

'Could be.' He walked with his hands thrust in his jacket pockets. Every now and then somebody spoke to him in passing.

'They'll all be saying, "Saw the laird oot wi' that bonnie lassie that's cam' to Briarybank"!'

Disconcerted, I managed to laugh at his exaggerated Scots accent.

'You can't move a yard in a place like this without everybody taking note.'

'Do you find that cramps your style?'

He flashed me a sidelong glance. 'It can make for problems!'

We had come to the river, upstream from where I had already seen it and we followed a walk along its bank.

'The Nether Burn,' he said, 'burn being the Scots word for stream.'

'It's more than a stream.'

'I believe the flow was increased last century to bring more water down for the mills.'

The river swung round sharply and I found we were approaching ruinous walls of red sandstone, in a wide stretch of well-kept grass. The foundation stones of walls no longer standing cut across the turf so that I could see that the original building had been on a grand scale. At some distance part of a wall was still intact with the tracery of what must have been a splendid window.

I said, 'I've seen this from the road.'

'The Abbey Church of Our Lady of Succour,' he said. 'Here where the river almost forms an island now was once all church and monastery, and over on the other bank they still come on bits of foundation walls when they're digging for new buildings. It was one of the great Border monasteries until you English burnt it at the Rough Wooing.'

'The Rough Wooing?'

'When Henry VIII wanted the baby Mary Queen of Scots for his son Edward VI. One of his charming methods of persuasion was burning the Border Abbeys.' He grinned. 'Your grandfather got very heated about that!'

'I resent your saying "you English" to me. From what I hear I'm probably more Scottish than you are!'

'Who's been telling tales?'

'Old Jessie Bruce gave me a history lesson yesterday. If you did come over with Robert the Bruce as she claims, then you're French!'

'The Dartie line—D'Artois.'

'That's the name on the portrait—' I stopped, aware that I was flushing painfully.

'In Briarybank, yes. The name died out in the 16th century. The D'Artois blood must be pretty thin by now.'

But the likeness in the portrait was strong! Surely he must have seen for himself!

He wandered between the foundation lines and I followed. At regular intervals were the bases of what had been great stone columns. He stopped, pointing out the nave and the choir. 'And on either side the transepts. Above us here was a tower with "A noble spire". I quote.'

'There are old records?'

'Oh yes. Clerkstoun, you see, was the town of

89

the clerks, or monks. It was the monks who started the wool trade, with their sheep on the hills and the river on their doorstep.'

The sun was low now and the light coming through the delicate tracery of the broken window burnished his hair. At our feet flat slabs lay embedded in the grass. The carved lettering was badly worn and the inscriptions were in Latin. It occurred to me that his earliest ancestors must be buried here. Beyond the solitary wall was a softening of trees. Yew trees, darkly green with gnarled trunks, trees as old as the abbey.

I shivered and he noticed. 'You're cold.'

'It isn't that. I just was so conscious of time.'

'I know.' He smiled. 'Let's have a cuppa! If you could bear ten minutes' walking up a vertical road I know just the place.'

He led the way across the river by an old stone humped bridge, and by back lanes to where the vertical road began. It was certainly steep, zig-zagging up the hillside between houses and gardens and rhododendron thickets. At last, panting, we reached the crest of a low hill and I found we had arrived under the terrace of an incredible building. It had everything—classical colonnades, medieval turrets, gargoyles on the highest gables. I gaped at it. 'Hillcrest Hotel!'

Keith laughed. 'Built by a Victorian mill-owner with an enthusiasm for all the architectural styles. There's even an Egyptian obelisk at the back! But as a hotel it's fine.'

We had tea in the lounge in a wide bay window that gave a panoramic view of the town. The tea was hot, the scones and the strawberry jam were home-made. The room was beautifully warm. As we ate Keith pointed out land-marks.

'The corn exchange, the haugh where the shows come—'

'The shows?'

'What you English would call the fair.'

'And what is a haugh?'

He was unkind about my attempts at pronunciation. 'A bit of low-lying land beside a river.'

I pointed to a large two-storeyed building with playing-fields. 'I suppose that's the school?'

'Clerkstoun Secondary, and very good it is.'

'And primary schools?'

'There are four.' He showed me where they were. 'Are you interested in getting a job in one of them?'

'No.' I hesitated. I had decided he was a friend. I had announced that I was staying on. I might as well come clean. 'I'm thinking of turning Briarybank into a school.'

'*What?*'

'For the pre-school age group,' I explained, shrinking at his tone. 'A sort of nursery school.'

91

'I see.'

'But you don't like the idea?'

He frowned. 'You'd have problems.'

'You mean there wouldn't be much demand?'

'There would be a demand. In fact great demand. There's very little for that age group.'

'But?'

'Well,' he shifted to face me squarely, 'is it practicable?'

'I've studied the lay-out of the house and I'm sure it can be done. I have a first-class teacher in mind to work with me—'

'Justin?' His eyes were expressionless.

'Heavens, no! He's a research pharmacologist. My flat-mate in Manchester. Her job has just folded and she might be persuaded to join me.'

He turned again to the view and was silent for a moment.

'It's rather far out of town,' he said. 'That could be a draw-back for young Mums.'

'I'd thought of that.'

'And the road itself—you might have trouble with the Council.'

'I'm not with you.'

'They could withhold permission if you were likely to cause congestion on a stretch of road that's narrow and twisting.'

'Oh.' I had not thought of that. There were difficulties at every turn!

'I could have a tactful word around?' he said.

Obviously he would know everyone. To have him on my side would be half the battle. But was he on my side?

'And on the whole question of a nursery school you couldn't do better than have a chat with Dave Mortimer. He's the local librarian. He was left last year with three youngsters under five and he has actually been trying to get something started. I'll fix that, if you like. And there's a friend of ours who might be able to advise on the domestic arrangements. I don't think you've met her—Antonia Crawford? She trained in household management and is thoroughly frustrated at home with her father in a house that runs like clockwork anyway.'

For some reason I felt less than grateful for the suggestion that his friend Antonia Crawford would be able to advise me on reorganising my house into a nursery school, but I had the sense to hold my tongue.

'How long are you staying?' he asked me after a bit.

'Justin is coming up for me on Friday.'

'What does Justin think of your idea for a school?'

'He thinks it's crazy.'

Keith permitted himself a smile. 'I can see how he might!'

Whether that was a reflection on my idea or on Justin I couldn't tell. Probably on both. The see-saw was tipping again. I felt my heckles rise. And so it was that I was short with him on the way back as I had been on the way into town!

That evening I did what I had shrunk from doing until now. I opened my grandparents' desk. It was full. There were bills going back for twenty years at least, all receipted and kept in elastic bands. There were bank statements, bundles of private letters, many of them with stamps I had thought of as interesting because of their age in my step-brother's album. There would be letters from my father, but I could not bring myself to look. There were no legal or insurance papers; these would be in the lawyer's keeping. And there was no sign of a document duly witnessed setting out any changed intention of my dying grandmother to overthrow the arrangements already made and will Briarybank to the man who had been like a son to her and my grandfather in their last years. Half an hour was enough. I locked the desk and re-wrote the latter part of my letter to Elinor.

'The plan is entirely feasible. Apparently there is demand for nursery school places in Clerkstoun. Of course there are problems. I shall need planning permission, for instance. But there are people who will help with advice and support. Would you consider joining me? For a bit, anyway, until you see how it works out? Think about it, my dear, and we can talk when I get back. Justin is collecting me on Friday, bless him! Much love, Lucy.' I next wrote to the lawyer, instructing him that I intended to keep Briarybank, and requesting that a valuation should be made so that the estate could be settled.

Then I started on the sweater for Elinor. The only sounds in the room were the ticking of the clock and the clicking of my needles. Evenings were long without television and record-player. The radio in the drawing-room wasn't working. Agnes had explained in an expansive moment that it had broken down in the last year of my grandmother's life and the old lady had refused to have money spent on it because she was too deaf to hear it! I began to think of bed and saw with a shock that it was just half-past nine. It was an enormous relief and pleasure when the phone rang.

'Hello there!' said Sarah. 'I'm ringing to ask if you're free tomorrow evening?'

'Oh! Well, actually I've promised to take in a concert between a candlelight supper and a fancy-dress ball!'

Sarah giggled. 'Now that's just too bad! I was going to ask you to come with us to *Tosca!*'

'*Tosca?*'

'It's an opera, Lucy, by a man called Puccini—'

'I know it's an opera, idiot! But how come *here?*'

'London and Manchester are not the only centres of culture in the country. The local Amateur Operatic Society puts on a show every year. They expect a party from Fenton. Dad really cares for music and would dearly love to pass on his ticket to you—'

'That doesn't quite make sense. If he dearly loves music—'

Sarah was enjoying herself. 'That's just the point! So you will come?'

'I'd love to, but I have no glad rags.'

'No problem there! I tell you what. Come over in time for tea. Estelle is just your size and she'll kit you out! Then we'll have dinner and make a grand progress into town.'

'Sounds an attractive programme!'

'There will be a party afterwards with lots of nice things to eat and drink—at the Crawfords' house. I'll pick you up about four then? Great! Goodnight!'

I had half-expected Sarah to arrive for me on Parsifal. I had not anticipated a slimline motorbike. We erupted out of Briarybank, tore up the hill and swept in through the wrought-iron gates of Fenton in great style. The noise was ear-shattering. We sent crows squawking, hens scuttling. I saw a cat shin up a tree. The Fenton dogs bounded at us from the terrace, tails waving, baying like a pack of hounds.

Mrs Fenton rose from a patch of heathers

that she had been tidying up for winter. 'Sarah, for one small woman you create an enormous amount of noise!'

We went indoors happily. Tea was set in the room at the back where we had sat on my previous visit. Colonel Fenton stayed to drink only one cup.

'I'm sincerely grateful to you for giving me an out tonight,' he said.

Sarah chuckled. 'Daddy plays the violin rather well and is blessed with perfect pitch. He claims that imperfect sound is torture to him!'

'The truth is,' he told me, 'that I'm off in a very few days now and I have to get organised.'

Soon after he left Keith and Estelle came in. Estelle looked as though she had just left a beauty salon. I found it hard not to keep staring at her. I had washed my hair that morning and had fancied that in the jersey two-piece I was wearing I looked quite smart. Now I felt all clod-hopper. She was as warm as ever and came straight to sit beside me.

'We're going to have fun after tea,' she said, including Sarah in her wide smile.

Keith sat near his mother and they talked together while we three girls chattered clothes and hair styles. Soon I was whisked away, up the grand stairs, by a great gallery to carpeted corridors and eventually to a lovely room all gold and white that was Estelle's. Here she opened wardrobes crammed with clothes. She took out one or two dresses, held them against me and shook her head.

'Too severe,' she said. 'Too old!'

Sarah sat cross-legged on the floor, her interest in transforming me switched off. She looked unhappy, her mouth set in a mulish line. Her father's going must be upsetting her.

I turned to find Estelle holding a dress towards me on a hanger. 'Try this!'

'Oh, that's not for me!'

'What do you mean?'

'It's lovely,' I said, 'but—'

She hustled me forward to a clear area before a long mirror. I looked at myself in the glass and I thought she would agree with me. The dress was magnificent, a kaftan with exotic birds and great flowers rioting over a champagne-coloured ground. It was simple enough. The neck was high, mandarin-style. The sleeves fell from shoulder to the floor. But the overall impression was over-splendid.

'You look gorgeous,' Estelle said. 'Sarah, come and look!'

Sarah came. 'Crikey!'

'Quite!' I laughed. 'It would be super if we were going to a grand function—'

'The point is,' Estelle said, 'that you look good in it. It emphasises your height and slimness, it brings out the colour in your hair. With a bright lipstick and eye make-up—'

'But not for tonight, Estelle. It's too much!'

'Too much!' She stood back, hands held up, fingers spread. For the first time I saw her as really French. 'It is a simple frock. There is nothing fussy. You will need no jewellery.'

There was an edge to her voice. I looked at the dresses on the rack. 'Please don't think me ungrateful, I'm not. It's just that—honestly, I'd feel over-dressed.'

She shrugged and ran nimble fingers along the rail.

'As you like. Try this?'

She held out a dress of limp plum-coloured crepe.

'The colour,' I murmured. 'It wouldn't—'

'No.' She riffled a moment more and then stood back. 'Do you see anything you fancy?'

I had had my eye on a simple cream-coloured dress with a square neck and three quarter sleeves.

'Could I try that?'

'Surely.'

Together we inspected it in the long glass. Estelle said nothing. She didn't have to. Subtly the dress didn't fit. The colour killed the lights in my hair and drained my cheeks.

'Sorry,' I said. 'You were quite right.'

I shared Sarah's room to dress for the evening. It was as unlike Estelle's as two rooms could be, and if my kaftan had looked wrong on me in the white and gilt setting it positively shrieked in this boyish room of books and sports things and great wall posters of remote corners of the earth. Sarah got ready mechanically and emerged looking fresh and pretty in green jersey trousers and a green and white top. She looked at me, wrinkling up her nose. 'You're quite something!'

'But you don't like it, any more than I do?'

She grinned. 'It's fun seeing you as a *femme fatale!*'

'Sarah, I'm not enjoying this and you're not being very helpful.'

'Sorry.' She turned away and stood by the window.

'It's your father going, isn't it? I do understand.'

'It's more than that.'

'You want to go too?'

She turned to face me and I saw with surprise that she was angry. 'I'm not a child. I may romp about and giggle a lot but I'm quite serious underneath, you know!'

'I realise that, Sarah.'

'Well, if you do, you're the only one who does! What I want to do with my life matters to me. I'm not being silly when I say I want to travel in difficult country. It's not romantic nonsense. I know too much about it to have any illusions.'

'You've been having a session about your future, I gather?'

'I'll say! Dad has got Mummy supporting the

100

nursing idea—'

I let myself down into a wicker chair.

'It's not a bad idea, you know. It's a first-class job in itself. You'd be good at it. And with nursing training—'

'I could get abroad. That's just what he said. Only I don't want it that way.'

'How do you want it?'

'Straight, as a man would.' She leant back against the window frame. 'I've thought a lot about what you said that night you came, about having a suitable qualification, like in geology—'

What had I done? A remark lightly thrown out, without support of real knowledge, either of her capabilities or career requirements. And what a career! A girl explorer!

'I've got good A levels. I've been sending out for University brochures. I've got the Application form from UCCA and it should be filled in soon. But Dad just laughed. He said, 'You wouldn't last a term at University. They don't let you keep horses in your rooms!' Mummy said, 'It was hard enough getting you to finish school'.'

'What would you want to study?'

'Well, actually—' She looked down at her twisting fingers—'I know it sounds frightfully erudite and unlikely, but I'm mad about anthropology and that got a lot of women into interesting places.'

'Why, Sarah, if you're really interested in anth—'

'Oh, I am! I've always been!' She pointed to her shelves. A glance along the book spines was enough. The posters spoke too.

'But they must know this surely? Your parents, I mean.'

The confidence died in her face. 'Not really. They have a picture of me, you see, as a kind of jolly, cuddly, unpredictable puppy. An *enfant terrible* who will one day grow up and become sensible. They enjoy things I do and say, to a point. But they're sure it's a fun thing, that I'll emerge out of. Dad could probably understand, but he's always been away such a lot and I was at boarding-school. Mummy's a dear, but she's a shade nervous of the madcap strain in Aunt Marianne and Daddy—says it's due to overbreeding. She's easier with Keith.'

'And what does he think?'

'About me?' Her tone had become bitter. 'I wouldn't know.'

I said gently, 'He's very fond of you.'

'He likes his horses too.'

'Sarah—'

She hunched away. 'He used to be the one who really cared. Oh, *he* never wanted to climb Everest or go to the moon. He is Border laird, through and through. Still, he seemed to understand. I could tell him anything. But now—' She stopped and shrugged. 'I thought at

102

first it was me, that I'd made him angry. But it isn't that. He's terribly unhappy, I think.'

My throat tightened. I didn't know what to say. The light had gone outside. Sarah drew the curtain over the black void.

'Let's go down,' she said.

Caught up in Sarah's problems, I had forgotten about my personal transformation and it was with shock that I met the family reaction when we entered the sitting-room. Colonel Fenton leapt to his feet, made me a sweeping bow and kissed my hand. Estelle and Mrs Fenton exclaimed and had me turn around like a model. Keith standing with his back to the fire looked startled.

Estelle said, 'None of *my* dresses fitted!'

'Come along, everybody!' called Mrs Fenton. 'Find plates and help yourselves. There are cold meats and salad and cheese and coffee.'

I held back with Estelle. 'You let them think this dress was *mine*?'

Her lovely eyes were all wondering innocence. 'Would that be so awful? It belonged to my mother and she let me have it for the material.'

There was no answer I could make to that.

All the discomfort I had experienced earlier returned tenfold. I saw that Estelle herself was elegant in a simply cut long woollen dress. Mrs Fenton wore a pretty blouse with a long skirt. I wanted to run upstairs and get back into my jersey two-piece, but the damage was done where it mattered. Keith was avoiding me and I could tell he was annoyed.

When we got into the car I sat in the back with Mrs Fenton and Sarah, while Estelle chattered brightly to Keith in the front. Sarah and her mother explained the arrangements for the evening. We would meet up with the Crawfords at the theatre and afterwards they were giving a party for friends who would include several of the cast.

'Antonia enjoys amateur dramatics,' said Mrs Fenton, 'but, not being a singer, she hasn't a part in this production.' She talked on about Clerkstoun's amateur theatrical group and I should have found it interesting, but snatches of conversation were reaching me from the front and they were even more interesting.

'Why on earth did you tog the poor girl out like that?'

'She's from the Big City, isn't she? That's how they'll expect her to look.'

'*They?*'

She said something I didn't catch. He said, 'Don't come that with me!' Estelle giggled. Mrs Fenton had asked me a question I hadn't heard. I bent towards her. 'I'm sorry?'

At the theatre all was bustle and excitement. There were bright lights and coloured placards and cars drawing up and people milling about in evening dress. I was introduced to so many people in the crowded foyer that it took me a little while to get clear just which of many attractive young women was Antonia Crawford. I got it straight at last as we sorted ourselves out and made for our seats. She was a tall girl, big-boned with a pleasant ease of movement. Nobody would have called her pretty, still less beautiful, but she had a clear skin, large grey eyes, a generous mouth that smiled readily, and I found myself liking her, although I hadn't wanted to. Her father was easy to talk to, a big man with thick white hair that set off the glowing tan on his face. Father and daughter had strikingly good teeth.

I had kept close to Sarah since we had left the car. Whatever happened I must have a seat next to her. The tickets, however, had not been taken in one row, but in blocks in the central area of several rows. Keith was in charge. There was a brief moment of confusion. I saw Sarah directed to seats with Mr Crawford and her mother. Another couple and a young man whose names I had missed were settled with Estelle and Antonia. And to my consternation I found myself with Keith in the two seats taken in the row behind the others. I was aware of some surprise, especially on the part of Estelle who turned and glared furiously at Keith, ignoring me. He grinned back, unabashed.

'Look,' I said, 'I know why you're doing this, and it's kind of you—'

'Mind-reading one of your gifts?' he quipped.

'You think I'm embarrassed in this damn' fool dress, and you'd be right! But I'm old enough not to let it worry me out of proportion—'

He was smiling and that line in his cheek was deepening. I hadn't seen him in formal clothes before. The jacket was well-cut. He was a man any girl would be proud to be seen with. I found myself blushing. Keep it sisterly, I reminded myself.

'Let's re-arrange,' I said briskly. 'I'd much rather sit with Sarah!'

'Well, thanks very much! Have you seen *Tosca* before?'

I faced him. 'Keith, please!'

He touched my hand lightly with his. 'I wouldn't say it was a damn' fool dress. Maybe a shade grand for Clerkstoun Theatre, but it brings out things in you that are muted in everyday garb. And why not dress up and give everybody a treat?'

'Then why aren't you wearing your scarlet-lined opera cloak?'

'That would dazzle you *too* much! Anyway I'd have had to pop it in the cloakroom with the top hat!'

I giggled.

'Do you know the plot?'

'No.'

'Well, there's this painter, Cavaradossi—he's

106

romantic and mildly revolutionary and tenor—'

'Naturally.'

'He is busy painting a church mural when he discovers a fellow revolutionary is in hiding in a side chapel, from the villain of the piece who is called Scarpia—'

'And is baritone.'

Keith nodded. 'Naturally. There's a bit of by-play with the sacristan, who is Dave Mortimer, by the way. I'll introduce you to him afterwards and we can make a date for a proper get-together.'

I placed him—the librarian who was interested in nursery schools.

'Bother,' said Keith, 'the lights are dimming. Not to worry! That should get you through the first bit.'

And it did. The lights were lowered, the orchestra started up, the curtain rose on another world, the dim interior of an Italian church. I do not play the violin, I do not possess perfect pitch. The playing and the singing sounded good to me. Cavaradossi, the tenor lead, was tall and dark and handsome. He threw back his well-shaped head and enjoyed his singing.

'You will meet him afterwards too,' Keith whispered as we applauded an aria. 'He's Clerkstoun's star lawyer.'

'A *lawyer*?'

Keith's face was close to mine. 'Why shouldn't a lawyer have a romantic persona? Or any man, come to that?'

I felt his shoulder against mine, and his arm pressed close. I felt the warmth of him and his nearness. In spite of his bantering protests he had sat with me out of kindness, but he was doing me no kindness. And the surging gloriously romantic music of *Tosca* was no help to a girl trying desperately to keep her feet on the ground.

CHAPTER FOUR

Tosca made her stately entrance, carrying a huge walking staff. Her proportions were ample but her golden voice more than made up for that.

'Not local,' Keith whispered. 'A foreigner from Edinburgh.'

I saw Estelle glance round, not for the first time. The lovers sang together well, although Cavaradossi could have done with longer arms. At a tender moment a fire engine tearing past the theatre with siren screaming sent a titter round the audience. I felt Keith laughing as I giggled silently. Then Scarpia was on stage, elegant, sinister with style to his singing.

'He's *good!*' I said softly.

'Runs a hardware shop down by the Abbey.'

The incongruity of it all, something in

Keith's tone had me laughing helplessly. He was laughing too. I choked and coughed. Estelle looked round again. Keith's hand closed over mine and for a moment I shut my eyes. I wasn't behaving very well or very sensibly. The first act ended with the Te Deum and the sinister Scarpia theme.

At the interval we had ices and moved around. Sarah was irritable. Obviously she wasn't having much fun where she was sitting.

Keith explained something of what was to happen in the second act, but it was complicated and I didn't take much in beyond the fact that, after fixing it with Scarpia that her lover's execution should be a fake, Tosca killed Scarpia. The acting flagged, the singers were tiring. I could sense restlessness in the audience. But the last act was glorious. The shepherd boy's soprano mingled with the music of Rome's Sunday morning bells. Cavaradossi sang his sad farewell to life and love. Then his Tosca came to him with her joyful news that he was to march out to a mock-execution. The handsome tenor walked proudly to face the firing-squad. Tosca watched him slump, seemingly acting well. But he hadn't been acting; she had been double-crossed. It was a tremendous moment of emotion, voices and music rising and transcending anguish as Tosca hurled herself from the Castel San Angelo to join her Cavaradossi in death.

We all clapped like mad and stamped our feet and the cast took curtain call after curtain call. It was an age before we got to the foyer and longer still to reach the cars. There had been some re-arranging. We had lost Keith and acquired Mr Crawford. Mrs Fenton drove. From the town the car went zig-zagging up and when we stopped at the Crawfords' house I realised it must be very near the Hillcrest Hotel. It was a fine house, of stone, built at the turn of the century in a restrained style. I had an impression of quiet luxury throughout, in the hall, in the bedrooms where we left our things. The drawing-room was washed in pale green with the paintwork white. Expensive rugs lay on the honey-coloured block-wood floor. The paintings on the walls were modern and interesting. I was studying them when Mr Crawford joined me.

'You knowledgeable about painting, Miss Lorimer?'

'Gracious, no! Very much of the "I know what I like" brigade!'

He smiled, flashing those brilliant teeth. 'Me too. I buy on the advice of a London dealer. As an investment. They say,' he turned to the near-abstract in pink and grey I had been looking at, 'that this chap Karinsky is appreciating already.'

'That's nice.' I wondered if Karinsky benefited.

110

'Of course, there's always a risk.' The light glinted on the metal rim of his stylish glasses. 'I've got something over here—' he drew me to a pair of flower studies. 'My dealer assured me I was on to a good thing when I bought these. And they are pretty, aren't they? You can live with pictures like these! But Litsen has plummeted. Nobody wants anything of Litsen's now.'

I felt a hand under my elbow and before turning I knew it was Keith. 'Lucy,' he said, 'I want you to meet the man who could be your keenest ally, Dave Mortimer.'

'How do you do?' I held out my hand. 'I did enjoy the opera. You must have had fun playing the sacristan.'

Dave Mortimer shook my hand and quite coolly set about sizing me up. Under the circumstances I understood he would have to, but it was disconcerting and I felt at a disadvantage in my *grande dame* dress.

He was of medium build, with a look of wiry strength. As the sacristan he had appeared elderly, but was probably in his late thirties. He had a strong nose, a lined forehead and large eyes under bushy eyebrows touched with grey. His mouth was firm over a firm chin, and he held his head so that he seemed to be considering me from an upward glance. I had no sense that he was reassured by what he saw.

Keith said, 'I've told Dave your plans. I'll

111

leave you to talk it over.'

He moved off with Mr Crawford. The cast were arriving. Cavaradossi was making a grand entrance to the congratulations of everybody around him. He was even more handsome close to than he had looked on stage.

'Well,' said Dave Mortimer, 'so you think you can turn Briarybank into a school?'

I brought my mind back to practical things. 'I believe it could be done.'

'You're an infant teacher yourself?'

'Yes. And the friend who may come in with me has many years' experience in nursery schools.'

'What age range were you considering?'

'Three to five.'

'And how many?'

'That would depend.'

'You've thought about facilities, I suppose? Toilets, fire rules, that sort of thing?'

I began to resent his manner but tried not to show it. Keith could be playing a devious game. He could be testing the seriousness of my commitment. This Dave Mortimer could in actual fact be an awkward customer and Keith could be doing what he could to head me off. My instinct to place absolute trust in Keith need not be a true one.

'I have given them thought, of course, but I'd need advice. I'm at the preliminary stage. First of all I had to know if there would be a demand

112

for a school like that.'

'Just why would you be doing it, Miss Lorimer?'

I bit back the retort I wanted to make. 'Because I would like to keep Briarybank and live in it, and I couldn't afford to keep it without making it pay its way.'

'I doubt if you would clear more than you could earn teaching in one of the town schools.'

That was a point I had thought of. There was no easy answer.

'But of course you wouldn't fancy that!'

'Where do you imagine I teach now?' I snapped. 'I work in an old red-brick building in a run-down part of Manchester. And I enjoy it!'

He smiled as if pleased that he had got under my skin.

'One point is that I could get tax relief on the use of my house in pursuit of my profession,' I said in tones as business-like as I could manage. 'The other point is that I want the house lived in and used, which it wouldn't be if I lived in it and had a job in Clerkstoun. There's a further thing—'

'What's that?'

I hesitated. It was something I cared about a lot. I could have told Keith, but I wasn't sure of this man. 'Briarybank is a wonderful place for children. It could stimulate the imagination—'

'Some of the little bleeders,' he said tersely, 'have their imagination stimulated enough

113

already!'

I wouldn't have believed that the sight of Estelle bearing down on me could have given me such pleasure and relief. Maybe it was because she had Cavaradossi in tow!

'Lucy,' she said, 'meet the hero of the evening!'

Dave Mortimer muttered something and moved away. I felt a thrill along the nerves as Cavaradossi took my hand in his and held it for a full minute. He was devastatingly good-looking. His hair was dark and well-cut. His features had the perfection of line and balance you seldom see. His eyes were grey, dark-fringed. He wore an elegant dark suit and a silk shirt with a saucy tie. He and Estelle made an exciting pair, and because they seemed to know it and take pleasure in the fact, my spirits rose. I didn't let myself analyse why.

'I shall call you Mario Cavaradossi,' said Estelle, 'until you get your part for next year. What will that be?'

'We're talking of doing *Il Trovatore*,' he said. His speaking voice was low and pleasing. He would make a soothing lawyer.

'In which case you will be?'

He smiled. 'If I'm lucky, Manrico.'

Estelle wrinkled up her pretty nose. 'Nice! But just in case Lucy wants to introduce you to someone who wants legal advice I'd better let her into a secret. He's called Alistair Logan!'

'Oh!' The let-down showed in my face and we all three laughed. 'Well, hello, Alistair Logan,' I said.

We talked about opera for a time. When I felt I should move on Estelle held me. 'Lucy is thinking of starting up a school. You could possibly help her? There are bound to be legal pitfalls—'

I wasn't sure that I could ever bring myself to discuss the details of loos per head with the exquisite creature I had watched loving his mistress and dying nobly before a firing-squad an hour before, but I mumbled something and he made an obvious effort to take an interest in my venture. I changed the subject as soon as possible and made another move to escape. Alistair Logan had had enough of a second female hanging around. But Estelle, thrusting her arms in his and mine, said,

'Let's go and grab some grub!'

We moved next door where a buffet supper was spread on a long table lit by candles. We passed Keith who was helping Antonia to cold chicken. Estelle chattered brightly. Her attention was mainly directed to Alistair Logan so that in the crowded room I missed much that she said. He seemed amused enough, rising well to Estelle's special brand of witty sex-sparring. But I saw him glance around from time to time and sensed he wanted to be elsewhere. Just what was Estelle up to, I wondered. I had been

115

so sure she was in love with Keith. Was she flirting with Alistair Logan to make Keith jealous? But that wasn't the way to get anywhere with Keith and she must know that as well as I did. And if she were hoping to vex Keith why should she hold on to me? I looked about me in growing discomfort. My face was aching from the effort of smiling. Sarah was with a group of younger people, laughing and obviously over her ill-humour. Keith and Antonia were standing by one of the tall windows, their backs to the room. Keith and Antonia! And Estelle minded. So that she had to have the hero of the evening at her side! But why have me along? Baffled, I stopped by a picture and pretended to examine it. Estelle and Alistair stopped too. Almost dutifully Alistair started on modern art. I longed to be away from this crowded room, clear of this tangled mesh of relationships which I couldn't hope to unravel. Then someone called to Estelle. She would have taken Alistair Logan with her and me too but we remained where we were. An awkward silence developed. I knew I should make an effort to keep the conversation going. So probably did he, but we were both too tired. The silence lasted a shade too long. I said, 'It's been a pleasure meeting you—' and he took his cue and moved away.

I looked for someone safe, preferably Mrs Fenton. She was in the centre of a laughing group. Sarah was still with her young friends. Keith and Antonia had left their window and I went to it, thankfully. The curtains were half-drawn and the window had been opened to let in some air. I leant forward, drawing in the sharp cold, hearing the sounds rising from the town. I could follow the streets by the lines of lamps. The moon was up and its pallid light touched the water of the Nether Burn. I could make out the river bends that formed the near-island with the Abbey ruins. I was aware of people passing behind me, talking, laughing, humming snatches from the opera. Someone stopped nearby but I didn't turn round. I had had enough of being sociable.

When Keith said, 'Tired, Lucy?' I couldn't believe that it was he who had been standing near me for some minutes. I turned slowly. 'Yes.'

'It's time we made a move, I think. If you make your farewells and get your things I'll round up our lot and meet you in the hall. Okay?'

'Okay,' I said and smiled the gratitude I felt. He smiled back. He looked strained, as though he hadn't had an easy evening. If Estelle cared for him, how could she bear to give him pain, a man like Keith who would take the hurt meted out to him as though he had deserved it and hide it away allowing no one near him to help?

Sarah sang all the way back in the car, out of

117

tune and in a kind of pseudo-Italian that I might have found funny at another time. Keith flashed past Briarybank and I hated myself for being there and having to give him the extra drive. At Fenton House they pressed me to come in for a nightcap but I stayed where I was. I had packed my jersey suit in a bag and had taken it with me just so that I needn't impose on them further.

'You've given me a wonderful time,' I said. 'I'll return your dress as soon as I can, Estelle.'

'Don't give it a thought,' she said. 'Any time will do.'

They stood on the conservatory steps and waved as Keith put the car round and drove off.

'I should have reminded you sooner to drop me off,' I said, but his thoughts would have been far away, my existence forgotten.

He took the Briarybank drive slowly and I realised it was to make as little sound as possible. He got out with me, took my key and turned it in the lock. I opened the door. Everywhere was deep silence. No owls were hooting in the high trees.

He said, 'I hope you enjoyed some of your evening.'

I stared up at his shadowed face. 'Oh, I did! I loved the opera.'

'I have a recording,' he said. 'You must hear it some time.'

'I'd love that.'

118

He brought up his hand and touched my face. His fingers were cold. My heart was thumping and I felt my bones turn to water. Was he going to kiss me? I willed him to, and I willed him not to. But he didn't kiss me. I had the feeling that he wanted to say something to me, but he didn't speak. Not for some minutes, and that is a long time. Then he seemed to gather himself up and said, very softly, 'Goodnight, Lucy. Sleep well!'

★   ★   ★

Next day I sponged and pressed the kaftan, packed it in a box with tissue paper and walked over to Fenton House in the afternoon. I went through the wood and round the base of the hill. It was shining again today not with frost but with sunshine on the wind-blown grass. I had not meant to call, simply to hand the dress-box in, but I had been seen. I found Antonia in the sitting-room with Estelle and Mrs Fenton. Everybody seemed genuinely pleased to see me and as I had nothing else to do I let myself be persuaded to stay to tea.

'Sarah is with her father,' said Mrs Fenton. 'He is packing up maps and guns and interesting things of that sort!'

We talked about his forthcoming trip and about Mrs Fenton's nieces and nephews for all of whom she had been acquiring presents.

When I rose to go Estelle jumping up said, 'I'll give you a lift. There's a tiresome tax problem that's been worrying me and Cavaradossi said last night he could help me with it!'

She was going to Clerkstoun to see Alistair Logan! I found it difficult to believe her tax problem was so urgent that she couldn't leave it for a time when she would be in town anyway. What was her game? Was she losing in her bid for Keith and setting herself to win the good-looking young lawyer? But it didn't make sense. Alistair Logan had not seemed particularly susceptible to Estelle's charms, and, half-French, with her looks and her nature, would she *want* to settle for a small-town lawyer, no matter how good-looking?

That evening when I was knitting her sweater, Elinor phoned. She is always brief, especially long-distance and she came straight to the point.

'I've had your letter. The school plan is on, then?'

'Well, yes.'

'Things are moving more quickly at this end than I had expected. I'll tell you all about it when I see you. But I won't go after anything else until we've had a chance to discuss your idea.'

'Do I take it you are in favour?' This was something of a surprise.

'It's worth looking at seriously,' she said, 'in view of what you've told me. I'll hold myself available meantime.'

She rang off before I had time to tell her of my doubts. But my doubts had nothing to do with the feasibility of turning Briarybank into a school . . .

About half-past nine Keith dropped in. He looked more cheerful and relaxed than when he had left me the previous evening.

'Coffee?' I asked. 'I'm allowed into the kitchen now!'

'Good for you! But thanks, no. I must get back.' He yawned suddenly and compulsively. 'I have some letters to write before I turn in. I was taking Antonia home. You saw her this afternoon, I gather. She stayed for dinner. And when I had dropped her off I looked in on Dave.'

'Oh yes?'

He lowered himself into one of the leather armchairs.

'You've got yourself an ally.'

I paused in the knitting I had picked up to give my hands something to do. 'Dave Mortimer?'

He nodded. 'Oh, he wouldn't give you any soft soap. I know our Dave. He thinks you've got a good scheme going. He thinks you have—wait a minute—"*mettle*"! You have a clear logical mind and you care for what you're

121

doing! There now!'

In spite of myself I felt absurdly pleased. 'But he was almost rude.'

'That's his way!' Keith stretched in his chair and I studied the pattern of his Aran sweater, wondering who had knitted it. 'He adored his wife. She was a wonderful little person, with a passionate selfless soul. When she died it seemed to us all that there was no justice in the world.'

'Has it made him bitter?'

'He wouldn't like to think it had. But yes, he's become more abrasive.'

'How old are the children?'

'The eldest is five now. The twins are three.'

'It must take a lot of courage to go on with what he was doing last night.'

'More than you think. Lena was their best soprano.'

'Oh, no!'

'She wouldn't have taken a part like Tosca. She was a Susanna for *Figaro*, Zerlina for *Don Giovanni*—You know the sort of thing. Yes, he's a brave man—'

Like you, Keith Fenton, I thought, watching him heave himself from his chair. And unsparing of self. With all he had to do, he had taken time out to see Dave Mortimer for me, and then report back.

'He would be glad to see you on Friday evening, if you could make it? Anyway here's his number. And he's with you.'

I followed Keith out into the hall. Justin would have arrived on Friday evening. Justin and Dave would not mix. I would have to see Dave sooner if possible.

'I don't know how to thank you for all your trouble—'

He cut me short. 'I'm tied up tomorrow morning,' he said. 'I've got to see Brydon who manages the Home Farm. But if you're free in the afternoon I have to go to the far side of the estate to look at a timber job. Would you like to come, see a bit of the countryside?'

'I'd love that.'

'You really don't ride?'

'The only horse I've been on was a wooden one in a merry-go-round!'

'We'll have to do something about that!' he said and laughed. 'For tomorrow we'll take the Landrover. There's a little loch I'd like you to see. It's got a little island with a ruined chapel.'

I didn't say anything because I couldn't. We seemed to stand silent again, smiling at each other for a very long time. Probably it was only for seconds...

It wasn't much use pretending any more. When he had gone I came back into the study and sat on the rug, placing my head on the leather chair where he had sat.

'Keith.' I murmured his name aloud, and the sound and the emotions it roused brought the

123

blood to my face and sent it pulsing through my body. So this was how it was, when you fell in love! The unimaginable joy, the pain of longing. I pressed my face into the shining leather. He's only being kind, I told myself, neighbourly, helpful. Trying to make up for seeming less than welcoming at first.

In the morning I walked early into Clerkstoun. It was a glorious day, with a clear sky and frost. I wore what I had planned for the afternoon's excursion, slacks and a thick sweater with an anorak over. When I called at the Library and was taken to Dave Mortimer's little office off the Reference section he didn't recognise me. At least not at first.

'Good heavens!' He got to his feet. 'Miss Lorimer!'

I laughed at the droll expression on his mobile face.

'The night before last,' I said, 'you saw me in borrowed plumes! I gather from Keith that you'd be interested in discussing the school project with me. I mustn't keep you now, but I felt I must look in to let you know how pleased I am to have your support. I can't make it tomorrow, I'm afraid. A friend is coming up from Manchester to take me back. My mid-term break is over, you see. But if we could keep in touch—'

He looked at his watch. 'Meet me for early lunch. There's a caff at the end of the road—pretty grotty but it's handy. We could establish a few facts and maybe, if Miss Bruce wouldn't mind, I could pop up one evening next week to have a look?'

'That's fine!'

'What's *she* say about the idea, Miss Bruce, I mean?'

'I haven't told her yet.'

'One thing's for sure. With her around you'd have no discipline problems!'

When we parted after our early lunch we agreed we had had what the telly reporters would call a 'useful discussion'. We had not seen eye to eye on everything. His biggest reservation was that the house was three miles out of the town. 'Then you say you have money for the necessary alterations. Fine! But I still don't see, unless you charge steep fees, how you are going to have any profit, once you've paid the salary of another teacher.'

That worried me too. Much would depend on Elinor. It could suit her, placed as she was, to work with me for board and lodgings for a bit, sharing with me anything that was over. But that presupposed a degree of selfless commitment I couldn't expect.

Keith had said he would pick me up at Briarybank and, afraid of keeping him waiting, I almost ran all the way back from Clerkstoun. He was pacing the drive when I rounded the dark holly bushes.

125

'I'm *sorry*!' I said and breathlessly explained where I had been.

'All right, all right!' Keith patted me down as he might one of the retrievers that waited grinning in the car. 'I've been looking at this drive of yours. These trees should come down anyway. I told your grandfather long ago—they're rotten. If you could make another entrance, so that you'd have an In and an Out, that could solve the problem of congestion on the road.' He showed me exactly what he had in mind. 'Then with lawn in front, you'd get more light in the house.'

'Marvellous,' I said, 'and I could have drifts of daffodils—'

His eyes twinkled as he held the door open for me. The wind tousled his hair. In wellingtons, with a leather-patched tweed jacket over cords, he looked rugged and fit. 'I hope you don't mind my bringing Rose and Cavalier. Father's organising his departure, my mother is supervising his organising, and Sarah is closeted in her room—"*working*", she says.'

We turned out into the road. The wind had risen and was driving puffs of cloud across the sky, with their shadows chasing each other over the rounded russet hills. The trees were entirely leafless now, their bark shining clear-etched in the sunshine.

'It would have been a lovely day for riding,' I said.

'You'll have to learn, then!'

The assumption that there would be other occasions sent me into a seventh heaven. I sat back in the Landrover, smiling from sheer happiness. He talked in a desultory way but I didn't really pay close attention to what he said. I heard the sound of his voice and watched his hands on the wheel and let myself dream. We left the motor road and bumped up a dust track in a long bare valley between hills. A brown stream came tumbling down through rocks, past rowan trees and silver birch. Sheep grazed on the hillsides.

'It's lovely,' I said.

'Too much bracken. And the heather's growing again.'

Near the head of the valley he suddenly jammed on the brakes and without a word leapt out, taking the dogs with him. I watched him go up the verge of a steep scree slope and stop where something grey showed at the foot of an outcrop of rock. He didn't stay long. I got out as he came striding down.

'Was it a sheep?'

'It was. A ewe.'

And in a month or two she should have produced lambs.

He reached into the Landrover. 'Like some chocolate?'

'Yes, please.' I didn't really want it. It would make me thirsty, but he was depressed about

127

the loss of his sheep and it would be churlish to refuse. We ate the chocolate in silence. I wondered what a sheep meant in money terms. In country like this he must allow for loss.

'If you'd like a drink,' he said, 'I would recommend the burn.' He sounded the 'r' in the way I loved.

'Say it again!' I said.

'Say what?'

'Burn!'

Our eyes met. He was laughing at me. 'Say 'loch'!' he teased.

'That's different. I can't!'

He caught my hand and we ran to the stream, Rose and Cavalier cavorting at our heels, grinning with their pink open mouths and lolloping tongues. Keith threw himself down on the grass beside a little pool formed from a gushing spurt of water, cupped his hands and dipped in his face and drank. He looked up, water dropping from his chin. 'Makes your teeth tingle!'

I followed his example and got very wet. The water was in my nose, on my chin, running up my sleeves, everywhere except where I wanted it.

'You can do better than that!' he said.

'Show me!'

He did. I managed a little better.

He began playing with the dogs, grasping their hairy heads, tumbling about with them. I got up and mopped myself dry. We walked back to the Landrover and got in. I found I was trembling and I hadn't thought it was cold.

From the valley head I got a brief glimpse into a lower broader valley, where a river flowed between woods, and houses showed white against thickets of evergreens. Our road swung south and we went higher. The grass was spare here, among protruding stone. The wind came whistling over the rise, catching the Landrover side-on. I was glad when the road began to drop. Soon we were well down, in a sheltered stretch between featureless sun-lit slopes. There seemed no end to it, this Border hill country. There wasn't a habitation in sight. Only the sheep and a few tattered crows moved in all the wide landscape. I became very conscious of Keith and of my being so totally alone with him. I had to talk and there was something I wanted to talk to him about.

'You said Sarah was *working*?'

'M'm.'

'She was telling me she had been sending off for University prospectuses.'

'Yes.'

'Don't you approve?'

'It isn't for me to approve or disapprove.'

I felt a prick of irritation. 'Surely you have thoughts about it?'

'Well, of course.'

'It's none of my business,' I said, 'but you

aren't being terribly helpful about it all. To Sarah, I mean.'

He shot me a sidelong glance. 'Did *she* say that?'

'No. But I'd say she'd welcome some advice.'

'I gather you've been giving her that.'

'Someone has to!'

'Advice without knowledge of all the facts—' He shifted in his seat. 'I'm sorry. You've been good to Sarah and I appreciate it. But she's not the studious type.'

'You might be surprised!'

'All this talk about being an explorer—She's got to live in the real world.'

'It's a wide world. There's no reason why she shouldn't get on expeditions. If she was equipped with the training expeditions might need.'

'She'd be more likely to meet with disappointment and heartbreak.'

'Your father didn't.'

'That's different.'

'Because he's a man!' My irritation sharpened. 'You'd think we were living in Victorian times, a girl like Sarah seeing her father go off to the Sahara or whatever, having to stay at home and arrange the flowers—'

'Nobody is suggesting Sarah should arrange flowers! We've got more sense! But she has to grow up, face accepting a job that is within her compass. Anyway she'll be married in a couple of years.'

'What makes you think that?'

'She's the type.'

'The *type*?'

I sat round facing him, my face flaming.

He said, 'She's lively and attractive and she loves people—'

'She would need to love *someone*, not just *people*. Anyway marriage is no alternative to a career. It's possible to manage both.'

'Oh yes?' His tone was dry. My heart was beating hard. 'I'm old-fashioned.'

I sat back with an exaggerated sigh. Sarah had said once that she could 'shake him and shake him'. I could now see why.

'Suppose I told you she is really keen to take a degree in anthropology—'

'She has always been keen on that. But there's a difference between a romantic interest and studying something for real.'

'You're *patronising* her! How do you know her interest is what you call *romantic*? How do you know she wouldn't enjoy studying seriously? Do you *know* Sarah?'

I bit my lip. I didn't need to look at him to know that I had gone too far. And I hadn't done Sarah's cause any good, either. He didn't speak, and I stuck at saying, I'm sorry.

We seemed to have reached the end of a long valley. Hills were closing in now, dark firs spreading over them in regimented blocks. I

131

didn't like them. They had the look of having been planted there as a crop, and then I realised that that was how it was. At a group of wooden buildings we drew up beside a flashy estate car.

'They've beaten me to it,' he said briefly, 'the timber people I came here to meet. I may be some time. If you feel like walking, take the dogs.'

He flung the Landrover door shut behind him and without a glance in my direction strode towards the timber building. In the back the dogs' hopeful rumblings quietened and they settled down to wait.

I sat for a few moments, with the windows wound down, smelling the pine resin, hearing the wind soughing in the trees. And then I got out. I opened the back door.

'Come, Rose! Cavalier!'

The golden creatures leapt down, rushing away and dashing back to me, sniffing at the ground, yapping their thanks for being let out. 'Walk!' I said. It was a word they knew. I got out the leads but didn't fasten them. They were well-trained. They were familiar with me now. Surely they wouldn't desert me on a private rabbit hunt! I followed a track that led into the forest. The tall spruce trees growing in close formation shut off the light except from the patch of sky directly overhead. There were signs that trees had been cut down recently, sawdust, piles of chopped branches, deep scores on the dark earth. Many of the trees had marks on them. Were they for the axe too? I knew nothing of what running an estate entailed. Keith had been doing it for years now. He must be knowledgeable about sheep and forestry, the condition of land and about river-control. He had mentioned someone who managed the Home Farm, which presumably would be arable land. I hadn't heard mention of a factor to supervise the rest.

Behind me I heard men's voices. Keith and the timber men were coming this way. I plunged down one of the forest rides, calling on the dogs who were drawn two ways. They settled for me, mercifully, and I walked on quickly. Soon I was wishing that I had left a trail, piles of cones or sticks to point the way. One forest ride is very like another and before long I was lost. I did not want to get back to the car too soon and so I risked taking a track that went up a slope. If I could gain height I would get my bearings. Eventually I reached a point where the trees had been cleared completely. It was a scene of desolation, as if it had been used for firing practice. I was able to see where I was, relative to the forestry huts. I hadn't realised the woodland was so extensive. It clothed the hills of all the near distance, in chunks of varying colour. The sun was bright, bringing out the resin smell. Here, sheltered from the wind, I was able to sit on a heap of logs. One of the dogs had found a rabbit hole and was excavating busily. The other was rooting happily in the undergrowth nearby.

I leant back and let myself think of Keith. How could I love him when I didn't know him? We were worlds apart, his values and all his life experience that had formed them so different from mine. He was the product of long generations who had cared for this still remote stretch of country, whose men had sometimes wandered, but whose women fulfilled their woman's function in the scheme of things. There were exceptions, of course. Marianne had broken free, but on balance she had lost out. Sarah didn't want to be caged, and probably would manage not to be. But Keith belonged. He and the Fenton estate were inextricably bound. He might be unhappy, his instincts as a man at war with what he knew he must do as laird of Fenton. But the laird of Fenton would win. He would not marry Estelle. The Colonel was right. Keith would marry Antonia Crawford. She would preside with her easy charm over Fenton House. She was in her element with horses and dogs—

Rose—or was it Cavalier?—had abandoned the rabbit burrow. I looked at my watch. It was time to move on down. I timed it well. The estate car was drawing away as I came out of the forest, with the dogs tirelessly nosing about me. Keith was talking to a tanned young giant whom I took to be a forester. When he saw me he lifted his hand. 'Won't be a moment!'

It took me more than a moment to get both dogs into the Landrover. When I succeeded at last and was about to close the door they saw Keith coming and bounded out to him. He punched their heads and they grinned at him in adoration and leapt at a movement of his hand into their place at the back.

'Humbling,' I said.

He got into the driving-seat. 'You managed them beautifully. I got a glimpse of you from time to time.' He sat back in his seat and let out a long breath. He looked tired. 'I just hope this lot give me a better offer than the last lot did.'

'Are you selling off timber?'

He ran his hands over his hair. 'Has to be done.'

'I saw a patch at the top where all the trees had been cut down.'

'Years old, that stretch. I don't go much for clear fell. Mostly it's thinning to leave room for trees to grow properly and selected felling which is a hell of a sweat.'

'That's cutting the trees that have been marked?'

'Yes. Young Alec there is a reliable lad but the selecting is something I have to do myself.'

He had walked every yard of those acres of forest, examining, assessing every tree!

He let in the clutch and we moved off. 'This

little loch with the island—'

'Look,' I said, 'I'm sure you've had enough.'

'Meaning you have?'

I was aware of that wry sidelong look.

'You know quite well I don't mean that!'

'How could I know, Lucy?'

Something in his tone set me trembling. If only I weren't so hopelessly vulnerable! It would be better if we could find something to argue about. But that was selfishness on my part. His need was for easy companionship, not a fight.

I said, 'Tell me about the island. You said there was an old chapel—'

There was not much known about it. It seemed that it was just there, a ruined chapel on an island in a remote Border loch. We came to it very soon, in a fold of the drowsy hills. The sun scattered silver on the water that was a hard blue and ruffled by the wind. We got out of the car and walked between high rustling reeds to where there was a boat. It took him less than three minutes to row across. The dogs leapt ashore, splashing in the shadows. He drew the boat up on the pebble beach and helped me clear the water. The island was rocky with patches of short turf between masses of whin. The walls of the chapel rose bleak and dank on the island's highest point. There was a simple arched doorway, two empty windows, grass where the floor had been.

We walked back the south-facing slope and sat down out of the wind. The grass was warm to the touch. Beside me Keith stretched his full length, with his hands behind his head.

'Funny,' I said, 'how islands are magic.'

He didn't answer. The water slapped against the stones, the wind moaned round the old walls. The dogs were quiet. One lay panting and grinning on the grass, the other sat alert, head on one side.

He said, 'What about a picnic?'

'Lovely idea!'

'Open up, then!' he said. 'I'll have a salmon sandwich to start with.'

I lay back on the turf. 'A sandwich? When there's cold chicken?'

'I bet you didn't put any tomatoes in!'

'I did, though. And there's ham—'

'And apple pie?'

'Apple pie!'

'I insist on having apple pie on picnics. And there's champagne. We could chill it in the loch—' He rolled over and lay beside me, leaning on one elbow. His head came between me and the sun, so that his face was dark and his head outlined with light. My bones melted. I stared up at him, helpless. I was far beyond reason or sense or rational thought. I loved him. I belonged to him for ever, body and soul. Didn't they say you heard trumpets? My lips parted. He must see I was trembling. His fingers touched my cheek, lifted a strand of hair from my forehead.

'Lucy,' he whispered.

Then I was in his arms, and he was kissing me, gently at first and then all gentleness went. He was lying over my chest so that I could hardly breathe. My hands were on his hair, that hair I loved. It was joy beyond belief, and pain too, all at once. His mouth was bruising mine. His skin was rough. And then he had let me go and he was on his feet. I heard him through the pounding of my blood.

'I'm sorry. That shouldn't have happened. You must forgive me.'

I sat up. He was striding down to where he had left the boat, the dogs at his heels. I watched him untie the rope where he had put it round a stone.

'Let's go!' He didn't look round. I struggled to my feet. I was too shaken to do more.

'Keith,' I said, but I doubt if he heard me. He jerked his head and the dogs leapt into the boat. I saw his hands on the bow. He was bracing himself to push off. I forced myself forward, not daring to look at him. He didn't help me in. He made a bad job of rowing back, keeping his head turned from me, growling at the dogs. Mercifully the wind was with us and it didn't take long.

In the Landrover it was a little easier. At least we didn't have to face each other. He drove too fast for the uneven dirt road. I was sitting with my face to the side window and when he drew up suddenly I went forward with a cry. But he didn't appear to notice. There was a man on the track, an elderly man with a weather-beaten face and a knapsack on his back.

'Professor Cairns! It's good to see you. Get in!'

I had the impression that this Professor Cairns had no great wish to abandon his hill-walk for a bumpy ride in Keith's Landrover but a natural shyness and punctilious good manners kept him from saying so.

I couldn't have told how Keith managed it but somehow the old man was soon seated between us and all the way over the hill tracks they talked, about weather lore and Border legend and ultimately philosophy. But I wasn't listening. Certainly I didn't take part. For one thing Keith hadn't acknowledged my presence. Only when he let the old scholar off on the main road did he remember something of the social graces.

'I'll have to leave you here, I'm afraid, Professor. I'm taking Miss Lorimer home to Briarybank.'

Even then he didn't speak to me. We turned in at the drive. A snazzy red car that I recognised stood on the gravel. From a garden seat in the sun Justin got to his feet, smiling.

CHAPTER FIVE

I watched Justin come walking over the gravel towards the Landrover. As if hypnotised I sat on. Keith, too, seemed unable to move. Everything in me clamoured, *Oh no, not now!* I needed time. I realised Justin was saying something and I got the door open.

'Well, Lucy Lorimer!' His smile went past me. 'Mr Fenton, isn't it? So we meet again!'

He was less townified than I had ever known him, in dark pants and a bulky sweater with a scarf tucked into the neck. His skin had a warm glow, with still a hint of that Adriatic tan. He had left his hair to tumble in the wind and it gave him a boyish look.

'I haven't been able to raise your retainer,' he said.

'Agnes—it's her day off.' I managed to get down, hoping he wouldn't touch me. 'You said Friday—'

Slight-seeming, he was tall, not much less than Keith.

'I pulled out all the stops and got away early.'

I rummaged in my shoulder bag and found my key. Keith had got down. He hadn't said a word. I turned to him. 'Would you like to come in? You must be gasping for some tea.'

'Thanks, no. I'll be getting along.' Avoiding

looking at me still, he faced Justin easily enough. 'I hope you have a good journey home.'

Did I imagine a light emphasis on the word 'home'? I didn't watch as he swung back into the Landrover. Justin made a thing of admiring the dogs, sounding knowledgeable. I hadn't imagined him able to tell the head from the tail. But Keith showed no enthusiasm for a prolonged chat. He started up the engine and had the Landrover round in seconds, narrowly missing Justin's scarlet treasure.

'Bastard should stick to horses!' Justin muttered. 'Aren't you going to let me in?'

I rushed to the kitchen, filled a kettle, got out tea-things, and, now that we were alone, prattling hard. 'Why didn't you ring and let me know you were coming? This is a poor welcome. Agnes always has Thursday off. There won't be anything much for supper—'

He lounged against the kitchen dresser, watching me, smiling. 'I'll have to stay the night. You don't mind?'

'Of course not!' If only he didn't get emotional and start kissing me. I said, 'You know what I'd really like?'

'What?'

'Let's go out! For dinner.'

His smile deepened. 'Getting tired of your house already, Lucy Lorimer?'

I carried the tea-tray into the drawing-room.

It was warm from the afternoon sunshine, although the sun was going now. I couldn't take him into the study and see him sit in the old leather chair. Not yet. I put a match to the fire and flopped on the rug.

'How is Elinor?'

'I haven't seen her. On the phone she was cagey. Admitted she had heard from you. I gather the school idea is still on?'

'You think it's nuts.'

'I didn't say so.'

'But you *do*!'

'Does it matter what I think?'

Did it? I was still numb.

'Do you mind driving back tomorrow?'

'Whatever suits you.'

'I mean, if you'd like to have the week-end in the country and all that—'

'I'm not so struck on the country, as you know.' He helped himself to one of Agnes's scones. 'And if *you've* had all you want—'

'I need to see Elinor. There's so much to discuss.' I set down my cup. 'Oh Justin, I don't know!'

It was a mistake. He was on the rug by me and in an instant with an arm round my shoulders and his face on my hair. But Justin was sensitive and in a minute he was back in his chair. 'Don't worry about it all, Lucy. You've been overdoing things, getting yourself in a fuss.'

142

'The school idea would work.'

'I'm sure it would. But don't rush your fences. We'll talk later.' He got up. 'I'll bring in my bag. I expect, if we're going on the town, you will want a bath.'

I looked at him, hoping the astonishment I felt didn't show. Was he always like that, considerate, kind, thinking of me? And did I take it for granted, so that I noticed it only now, after we had been apart?

It is possible, with an effort of will, to shut things away, to close a door in the mind, and that is what I did now. I put it all from me, the afternoon with Keith, the fierce joy and the searing pain, and lived only each moment as it came. When I had shown Justin to the room Agnes had put ready for him I didn't take the bath I craved. There I would be alone too long, I might let go. I washed briskly, changed into the blue woollen dress with its gold chain for a belt, brushed my hair, put on some lipstick and clattered downstairs. I washed up the tea-things, put up the fire-guard in the drawing-room and was writing a note for Agnes when Justin joined me in the kitchen. He had changed into a suit I hadn't seen before in a soft green weave.

'Smart,' I said.

His surprised pleasure touched me. He said, 'Where shall we eat? Should I phone and book?'

'In Clerkstoun? You must be joking.'

'Still think it's a dump?'

With fine things. I turned away quickly. I had been so sure that I was all right. I couldn't go to Clerkstoun any more than I could sit out the evening in Briarybank. 'There's a place I've heard about—it's quite a distance from here, on the Edinburgh road—'

'Fine,' said Justin. 'Shall we go?'

Darkness had come down. The nights were closing in, winter had taken over from autumn. We ran quickly into Clerkstoun and out again. I had seen no more than a blur of lights, bunches of young men on bikes milling round the cafés. It could have been any town. I asked Justin how his research work was going. He hadn't ever attempted to explain it to me, certain that I could never have understood it or felt real interest. Sometimes I had wondered if he were really all that interested himself. But he enjoyed talking personalities, relating the little feuds and confrontations. He could be amusing when he chose, and tonight Justin chose.

We reached the restaurant sooner than I had expected. Justin had been driving fast. It was a flash place, with soft lights, piped music in the bar, arty décor with an occasional claymore or swathe of tartan to remind the tourist he was in Bonnie Scotland.

Justin was taken by surprise. 'Set down in the midst of nowhere? What's it called? The Border Mill?'

'They say the food's good. People come out from Edinburgh.'

It was Estelle who had mentioned it, talking that evening with Alistair Logan after *Tosca*.

Justin organised a table for dinner and we settled in the bar. For almost the first time in my life I felt the better for a drink. That little door in my mind didn't stay shut too well and I had experienced several bad moments on the way. Now I was able to chatter. A second drink put everything at a certain distance and I could give Justin some account of what I had been doing. We went in to dinner. The food was good. Justin ordered a bottle of sparkling rosé. I was relieved to find him refraining from cheap jibes. I couldn't have taken remarks about my land-owning neighbours or my aristo. Inevitably we worked round to my plans for a school. At first he was not for expressing a direct opinion on the scheme. After a bit, studying his glass gravely, he said, 'Well, it's difficult for me. My position is prejudiced.'

'What do you mean?'

He raised his head. In the soft light his eyes were very dark. He was smiling gently. 'If you go ahead and turn Briarybank into a school, I lose you.'

I found myself trembling again. He must have seen.

'The last thing I want to do is influence you or upset you. You must do what you want to do.'

I found it difficult to finish the Bombe Jeanne d'Arc.

He said, 'Let's have our coffee in the lounge. I've been hearing electronic sound. Do you think there's dancing?'

Dancing was the last thing I wanted, and yet in the lounge with its muted lighting and the strident music I had a refuge from any need to talk. A few couples were on the floor. I watched them dully, from a kind of paralysing ache.

When at first Justin said, 'Shall we?' I shook my head. Then the group went into a number we had danced to in Manchester discos and he stood up. On the floor it wasn't so bad. I gave my body to the music. The door closed in my mind. Justin was an exciting dancing partner. I was conscious of people watching him, admiring his virtuoso performance. And he was high-spirited with it. In spite of myself I followed his lead. Soon I was laughing. When he drew me close to a slow romantic tune I felt myself beginning to relax, some of the pain seeping away. He put his cheek against mine and softly whispered the lyric. It was the usual trite stuff: 'You are my life, my love—' but I knew that, singing it, he was finding a way to say what I hadn't given him the chance to put into his own words.

It was not so very late when he suggested we had had enough. He had his arm round me when we crunched over the ice-crisp gravel to the car. In the car he kissed me lightly. The moon had risen in a frosty sky clear of cloud. The pallid light lay on the rounded hills and whitened the skeletal trees. We were some miles short of Clerkstoun when he drew off the road and stopped.

He sat back, smiling at me. 'Lucy Lorimer, relax! I'm not going to force myself on you if you don't want me!'

'Oh, Justin!' After the day I had had his kindness was too much. I turned to him and dropped my head on his shoulder. His arms came round me only slowly and he made no move to kiss me.

'I do realise what I said back at the Mill was fairly stark. But I had to say it. You do see that, Lucy?'

'Yes,' I whispered.

'It's a funny thing being in love. It doesn't happen that one day you're not and then the next you are! I suppose I knew it was always there as far as I was concerned. I didn't know how you felt. I thought we had time. And then this house of yours happened.' Briefly he brushed my forehead with his lips. 'That's why I was snappy to you about it, I suppose. I couldn't help seeing what it could do to *us* if you wanted to keep it. And it brought to a head just what *us* meant to me.'

I held myself motionless.

147

'It would be a bit presumptuous of me to say "Sell the damn' place and marry me!" It's something you have to think about.'

His generosity shamed me. He was offering me all he had and I was leaning against him drawing comfort from him, offering nothing.

I said, 'I'm not in love with you, Justin.'

I felt him stiffen. For a long time we stayed as we were, and then he pressed my head closer in to his shoulder.

'I know. That's why I haven't spoken before. I felt I had no right.'

But what, I wondered in bitterness and pain, was love? This fierce aching longing for Keith Fenton that filled my whole being and deadened me, cutting me off from hope of happiness anywhere? Was I to give in to that, surrender myself to a hopeless passion for someone who had made it clear that he didn't want me? Pine for a man who kissed me out of frustrated love for someone else? This infatuation with Keith Fenton could poison my whole life, could send me down wrong paths, away from life as I should lead it.

I prised myself up, wiping my eyes for I found I had been crying. 'I'll have to think, Justin.'

'Of course.' He sat without looking at me, in a kind of dignity I hadn't met before. There were depths in Justin I hadn't suspected. How would I have felt if he had talked of love in this way a few weeks earlier? Before I came to Briarybank and met Keith Fenton? Wouldn't I have been happy and grateful for the love of a man I was fond of?

He put his hand on mine and squeezed it. 'You're tired. I'll get you back.'

We scarcely talked all the way back to Briarybank. The moonlight revealed the familiar countryside. This time passing through Clerkstoun I could see the ruined Abbey wall with its blind window, the leaden water of the snaking Nether Burn. I saw the hills that enfolded my home, the cathedral of beeches, the dark holly mass.

Agnes had left coffee in a thermos jug and some of the shortbread biscuits that she knew I liked in a tin box.

'We'd better try to take something,' I said. 'Otherwise she'll be hurt.'

'Does she have feelings, then?'

It was the first snide remark he had made and he instantly apologised for it.

'She *is* a good soul,' I said forgiving him, 'but it takes time to find it out.'

The kitchen range had been cold for some time. There was nothing for it but to switch on the electric fire in the study. I watched Justin sit down in the chair Keith had sat in. It didn't matter.

'Agnes has been kind,' I said, 'in her way. Everybody has been kind—'

149

'But?'

I stood at the window, drawing the curtain aside so that I could see my hill in the moonlight.

'I'm a newcomer.' As I spoke I realised I didn't wholly feel that. There was much I didn't understand. But that was something else again.

Justin said, 'It's understandable you should feel that. This is a rural community. Let's face it, a bit of a backwater. They can't have changed their ways much in a hundred years. You've lived all your life in London and Manchester.'

And I wanted to live the rest of my life in this backwater, among the gentle Border hills, with Keith seeing to his sheep and his forests and his land. But this was a dream that could never be fulfilled. Would anything else be other than pain for me? Feeling for Keith as I did, would I ever find life at Briarybank bearable? After what had happened between us would my staying on here be fair to him?

'The trouble is,' I said, 'I've committed myself on the school.'

'In what way?'

'Well, Elinor, for one. Her job had folded and she has promised to come up and see what I've got in mind. I'm frankly surprised. I'd have expected her to be more cautious, but she sounds positively enthusiastic.'

Justin smiled wryly. 'I can think of several reasons why she should.'

'Oh yes?'

'Jobs aren't so easy to come by these days—'

'*She'd* have no problem.'

'Living here could suit *her* very well. And she would love to prise you out of my orbit.'

'*What?*'

'She hasn't ever liked me.' He grinned. 'I can't think why! Maybe it's because she hasn't a boyfriend herself!'

I held my hands to the electric bars. Elinor would judge my school plan on its merits.

'There's a man here, Dave Mortimer, the town librarian. He's a widower with three small children, and is very keen to see something started for the pre-school age group.'

'Does Elinor know about him?' Justin asked brightly. 'Maybe *that's* why she is so enthusiastic!'

'I have a feeling, Justin, that you are being less than sympathetic.'

'Sorry, my dear.' He put out his hand and lifted a strand of my hair. 'Just trying to cheer you up in my own inimitable naughty style! I doubt if either Elinor or this widower-librarian would regard anything you have said so far as binding.'

'Then there's the lawyer—I've written him, telling him what I was planning, asking him to proceed with a valuation on the basis that I won't be selling.'

'There's nothing to that. His job is to carry out his client's instructions.'

'But I can't go on chopping and changing.'

'It's a lady's privilege!'

'Against all that, there's something else.'

'What's that?'

I hadn't meant to be so frank with Justin, but I had to have someone to confide in. 'Keith Fenton was like family to my grandparents. He looked after this place for years, since they got too frail to cope themselves. He must have thought—I mean, I can't help wondering—'

Justin leant forward but I avoided looking at him. It wasn't easy to talk about Keith Fenton. 'Well?'

'I have the idea that my grandmother, before she died, may have made another will in his favour.'

Justin's shocked reaction was entirely genuine.

'But that's preposterous!'

'Is it? After Grandfather died my grandmother got to depend on him more and more. She hadn't seen me for fifteen years. He—he loves Briarybank. She must have known that.'

'But the lawyer would know about any will she made.'

'Not necessarily. She was wandering in her mind towards the end—'

'In that case, a will would not be valid!'

'I don't mean "wandering" in the sense that she wasn't in command of her faculties. Just forgetful—'

'But a will has to be witnessed.'

Justin had really got his teeth into this! 'I know. But she needn't have had Agnes or anyone very close. She could have called in the postman or asked the district nurse.'

'They'd have known what they were doing. There would have been talk.'

'There could have been, for all I know.'

Justin heaved himself out of his chair. 'Okay! Let's say the old girl made another will! Where is it?'

I looked at him helplessly. 'It could be anywhere in this house. That desk, for instance, is stuffed with papers.'

'You've been through it?'

'No. I gave it half an hour one day. I couldn't take any more.'

Justin tugged at a drawer. It was locked. I poked around in my bag and threw him the keys. 'I can understand you wouldn't enjoy a job like that!' He placed the keys on top of the desk and came back to the leather chair. 'Supposing you found a will in Fenton's favour, what would you do?'

I turned from his searching look and bent to the fire. What would I do? Present it personally to Keith, see the expression naked in his face

153

before he could cover up? No. I would send it to the lawyer. But I would not wait on the due processes of the law. I would move out straightaway, leaving him to make his choice among the women clamouring for him, with a house all ready to dump his mother and sister.

'Well, if that's the way of it,' said Justin who had been watching my face, 'shouldn't we make a thorough search now?'

Weariness dragged at me as I got to my feet. 'I suppose we ought to check seriously before I go any further. Tomorrow, in the morning, before we leave. Could you bear it?'

Justin was on his feet beside me. 'Surely!'

'I wish that I could find another will!' The words seemed to come without my volition.

'So that you could be clear of it all, Lucy Lorimer? Without having to make any tiresome decisions. Well,' he smiled gently, 'maybe we shall! Now—*bed*!'

He locked up while I rinsed the thermos jug and washed the cups. Then we climbed the stairs together. My feet trailed as we reached the top. I kept my face turned from the portrait in its gilt frame. I prayed that Justin would let me go, without goodnight kisses and a demonstration of affection I was too numb still to feel. He stopped by my door.

'Goodnight,' he whispered. He dropped a kiss on my cheek and touched my hand and then went on along the corridor. Agnes, old-fashioned that she was, had put as much of the house between us as she could! I had been longing for bed because I wanted to be alone. I had not expected to sleep at all. But after a brief storm of bitter sobbing I slumped and sleep must have overtaken me quickly. I came awake suddenly and lay wondering for a disorientated moment where I was. It was black dark outside. The moon had gone down. My heart was thudding as though I had had a fright, and yet no vestiges of nightmare remained in my consciousness. I tried to rid myself of a nagging unease. I told myself I must have been dreaming. Even in sleep I had been protecting myself from pain and I had wakened rather than face up to the truth of what lay ahead for me—life without a hope of love as I now knew it could be.

I turned over and tried to shut the door in my mind. But now in the ebbing small hours the door wouldn't be shut. I put on the bed-lamp. Three o'clock! I had a long difficult day before me and I needed to sleep. A hot drink might help. I lay in bed and thought of cocoa. Reluctantly, because out of the bedclothes it was cold, and making cocoa required effort. But without a hot drink I should never drop off. I would lie here turning about, hour after hour, I'd have a headache in the morning. I got up, put on dressing-gown and slippers and made my way downstairs.

Part of me was probably still asleep, and if I hadn't heard a sharp cracking sound coming from the study I should probably not have noticed that there was a light showing beneath the study door. I stopped and considered. I could have left the light on. I could well have imagined the noise. But the light would have to be put off. In a kind of part-awakened state I pushed the door open. Certainly I could not have coped if I had been faced with a burglar. As it was, when I saw Justin at my grandparents' desk, bundles of letters and papers set out on the floor beside him, I didn't at first realise anything was wrong. If Justin had had the wit to take me by the shoulders and steer me back to bed with comforting words, I might just have obeyed. Part of the way, anyway. But the look on his face jerked me fully awake. He crouched, like a wild thing, his elbows out as if protecting treasure trove from someone who threatened him.

'Just what are you doing?' I asked him, and then I knew. 'Saving me the morning's work? How kind of you, Justin!'

He was recovering as I was coming to life. He straightened.

'That's right, my dear. I wanted to save you a distressing hour or two—'

'Like hell you did!' I saw a box of matches in a tin lid on the end of the desk. 'And you haven't found a will? And we wouldn't have found one in the morning, Justin, would we?'

'What are you on about, Lucy Lorimer?'

'Don't Lucy Lorimer me! You were looking for another will, weren't you?'

'Right!'

'And you were going to burn it if you'd found it. Weren't you, Justin?'

'For the love of Heaven—'

'Not for the love of Heaven, Justin! Not even for the love of me. For the love of *you* Justin Wain! So that when I was sucker enough to say I'd marry you, you'd be getting a girl with over twenty thousand pounds to her name! Only twenty thousand or so, Justin. Had you forgotten the spectre at the feast, our friend the Tax-man—'

'You're raving! Here I am, down here in the cold, trying to help—'

'Cut it out! Don't be so cheap! You put on a marvellous act yesterday. You're quite sensitive when you choose to be. You never put a foot wrong and I fell for it. Hook, line and sinker, because I was tired and miserable—'

His wide smile flashed out. 'Miserable, darling? After a day out with your rugged aristo—'

'Be *quiet!*'

'I'm sensitive, all right! I felt the vibes! Fancy him, don't you? And he won't play? But maybe if you could find a will and gave it to him and he got your precious Briarybank—'

157

'How dare you! How dare you talk to me like that! *Get out!*' Choking with rage I advanced on him. I must have had something of a medusa look for he recoiled. 'Get out of this house! Out, I said, *now*! Yes, now! Get up those stairs and pack your things and take yourself and your car out of my sight!'

From over the desk he faced me. He was pale, his eyes very bright. 'You little fish-wife, you! D'you imagine I ever gave one damn—'

'I don't imagine anything!'

'What will you do if you can't find a will to hand to him? Go to him and just say "My house is yours" like they say in Spain!' He threw up his arm like a Spanish dancer, snapped his fingers and cried, 'Olé!' And then his eyes slid past me and he lowered his arm. I wheeled round. Behind me Agnes stood with a heavy torch in her hand. She stepped aside from the door and without another word he sidled through it. I heard him run lightly up the stairs. Agnes bent and switched on the electric fire.

'Stay here and keep warm,' she said. 'I'll see him off the premises.'

I bent over the fire, hugging myself to stop shivering. My teeth were chattering. The blood was thudding in my head. Dear God, was there no refuge anywhere? Justin had seemed so kind, and I had been so grateful. And it had all been sham. He had been playing his own game, cleverly by ear, each stage at a time. He had probably liked me as much as he would ever care for anybody. When I had got my inheritance I had become seriously desirable. It must have thrown him when I had announced my plan to keep the house and run a school. But he had been skilful. He had had no illusions about what I felt for him. He hadn't tried to argue for love then. He had given me time to find turning a house into a school was not all that easy. Just when I was coming to grips with the snags he had staged his re-appearance. And he had been luckier than he could have dreamed of. He had caught me on the lowest emotional down-swing, when I'd have run to any refuge from the bleak realisation of my hopeless love for Keith Fenton. Last night he could afford to act the perfect gentleman and play it cool. He must have felt he had me and my legacy all wrapped up and tied with ribbon. Only then the tiresome lovesick little fool had started maundering on about another will—How he must hate me!

He was on his way down now. I could hear Agnes turning the outer lock. I felt the icy draught along the floor but I couldn't make the effort to get up and shut the study door. I heard his steps crunching on the gravel. Agnes must be waiting to see him drive off. The night was arctic cold. The car engine started up, faltered, fired again. I heard the tyres move on the drive. Agnes slammed the outer door shut.

It was then, I think, that I started to cry. Agnes left me to it. In minutes she was back with strong hot tea. I sipped it. I couldn't very well have said that I'd prefer cocoa. She returned from the kitchen again, this time with a hot water bottle in her arms.

'Come on, now, my lass. Come away to your bed.' She walked me up the stairs and into my room. 'Now just make sure that electric blanket is switched off. If the bottle leaked you could electrocute yourself!'

She fussed about me, tucking me up. Then she switched off the light and left me. Incredibly I slept, and woke to find the room flooded with sunshine and Agnes placing a tray on a table at my bedside. I sat up in bed. 'You should have roused me,' I said. 'I can't have you pampering me like this!'

It was a grim smile that Agnes produced, but definitely a smile. 'You could do wi' a bit o' pampering. Now eat this while it's hot.'

As I had discovered earlier in the week Agnes's breakfast bacon was delicious. 'I don't know how to thank you,' I said. 'For everything. And now I'm not certain just when I'll be leaving. You see, I shall have to go through my grandmother's papers. I should have done so before, I know, but somehow—'

'You needn't waste your time.'

I looked at her where she stood arranging the curtains to her liking.

160

'As far as anybody else is concerned, Miss Lorimer, what took place last night never happened. But between you and me—well, I couldna help hearing a wee bit. It does you credit, wanting to make sure there wasn't a will left in Mr Keith's favour. But no such will was made. Your grandmother and me—well, we talked about it, you see. At the end she treated me like a friend. She wanted Mr Keith to have Briarybank. She thought plenty about altering the will that she and your grandfather had drawn up. But it would not have been what the old man wanted and she could not bring herself to do it.'

I gazed at her straight back in the stiff brown frock. How much simpler and easier it would have been for Agnes if my grandmother had altered the will! There wouldn't have been the fear of moving out with her old mother when the house was sold. For with the spec builder in the market there could be no certainty of Keith Fenton going to a figure that would secure him the property.

'Had you heard that I was seriously considering keeping on the house? That I was thinking of turning it into a school?'

'There's been a bit o' talk. But I knew that you would be telling me what you had decided as far as it affected my services in your own good time.'

'Oh, Agnes!'

161

She turned round then. 'You haven't finished your bacon!'

'I've been so uncertain. I love the house. It *could* be made into a school. I've been sort of taking it for granted that if I went ahead with my plan you would stay on? Your mother—well, it would be hard for her to leave the house where she's lived most of her life—'

'We would not be looking for special consideration. Your grandparents provided for my mother. I can find work in Clerkstoun. If I stayed on here with you, Miss Lorimer, it would only be if you wanted me and if I was agreeable!'

I stared at her.

'We have never been known to take any kind of charity.'

'I appreciate that. It—it would be a great kindness to me,' I said, 'if you would stay on.'

'You're keeping the house, then?'

I pushed the tray from me and brought my head down on my knees . . . 'Agnes, I'm still not *sure*! Last night I had pretty well decided not to, and now—' She took the tray from the bed. I was aware of her standing stiffly, holding it. 'I have to get back to Manchester tonight if possible. I start work on Monday.' I looked up at her, surprising a kindliness in her eyes that I wouldn't have believed possible. 'I wish,' I said, 'you and I could have talked sooner.'

She bent her head. 'Aye, maybe. But it's no'

my way.'

'You mean you had to get to know me first?' I wondered how much she had heard the previous night. Now, she probably knew me far too well!

'I tell you what I'll do, Agnes. There's a train from Edinburgh around five. That means I can have a bite of lunch here and catch the half-past two bus. I'd been planning to ring Miss Sarah and Mrs Fenton before I left. I'll have a walk first, try to get myself sorted out.'

It was a relief to be alone. I lay back in bed, heavy with lethargy. I needn't pack yet. There wasn't much. Sunshine streamed in through the high windows and lay across the floor. I could see the bare branches of beech trees, the smooth bark shining in the light. There was a great chattering among the birds. The cat from the cottage must be on the prowl. I thought of hostile-seeming, enigmatic Agnes who had proved such a support. Should I feel such surprise? Keith was fond of her. I ought to have known. Keith! I turned my back to the window full of the sparkling morning and shut my eyes.

What to do now? Last night everything had become simple. I would go back to Manchester with Justin, to the old familiar life. I would let Keith become a memory of another world as the portrait of my knight had lost all reality in a child's dimly-remembered fantasy. But now Justin was horror. I shrank from the very

163

thought of going back to places where I had been with him, places where I might meet him again. My instinct was to stay here among the hills, with my work, in my house. I would be busy enough. Once the school was under way I would not have the leisure to go about. Once Sarah had started on whatever course of study she settled for, I need have only the slightest and most formal contact with Fenton House. The memory of those moments by the loch would fade, they would be seen by both of us for all they were—a brief madness between an unhappy man and a girl with too much of what Agnes would call 'nonsense' in her head.

I swung out of bed. I would have a last walk before catching the Edinburgh bus. I dressed for travelling, in slacks and sweater with a warm jacket. I looked into the kitchen on my way out. Agnes was baking.

'You're looking more cheerful, Miss Lorimer! I'm making some shortbread for you to take back with you!'

I checked an impulse to go to her and hug her. She wouldn't like that, ever, even if we worked together for years and became, as she and my grandmother had been, friends. 'Thank you,' I said. 'I'll be back by twelve.'

I crossed the stream and started up the Shining Hill. Here the morning was less bright. Mist hung in layers with the sun filtering through in a haze of spun-gold. I was somehow deadly tired and abandoned the idea I'd had of climbing the hill. Where should I go? Everywhere as far as the eye could see was Fenton land. The last thing I wanted was to meet my knight on his charger! I followed the stream where it cut a meandering way through silver birches and winds well clear of the woods around Fenton House. The stream joined another and with the increased water broadened out. There was a sweep of gravel where the walking was easy and I picked my way on that and on the larger stones in the stream's bed. The water was clear, with every pebble sharply defined. There was no wind today. The sheep grazed placidly. Curlews wheeled in the sky, crying. Gradually my weariness left me and I was moving at a good pace. There was no need now to shut doors in my mind. It was as if I had been through the fire and had emerged, scorched certainly and aware of pain, but conscious that I had known the worst and could cope reasonably with what lay ahead. A time would come when I would be happy again. Justin's despicable behaviour had saddened me, more the calculated sweet reason with which he had played me the previous evening than his more spectacular villainy over the will, but against that I had found good-will in Agnes where I had believed it would never spring. And while it seemed odd to set the one against the other yet I found myself doing just that and drawing comfort from it.

I left the stream and followed a zig-zagging track that took me past a belt of spruce to the top of a squat hill. Here I could scarcely believe my eyes. At what seemed no distance, surely not more than a mile away, lay the loch with the island. I stood and gazed at it, measuring the distance, judging the time I had. Did I want to visit it again anyway? Without conscious decision I dropped down from the squat hill, crossed a valley and breasted a scree slope leading to a rocky ridge. Try as I might, I could not see the dust roads by which we had driven in the Landrover. They would have been made, of course, to give vehicle access to pasture for winter feeding and to forest and would not follow the shortest route.

I could now see the folding acres of black-looking spruce woods where Keith had met the timber merchants. The ridge had seemed innocent from the valley, a mere stretch of high land narrowing at its summit, but when I came to cross it I found I was on rugged rock. Thankful there was neither wind nor ice, I clambered over the serrated edges, letting myself down between slabs of rock clammy with lichen and cold on the sunless side. When a piece of rock that I was holding broke off in my hand and I felt myself slithering I was not greatly worried. Nothing was happening fast. I put out my hands to slow my slide and my concern was wholly for my gloves. I put out my feet ready to balance myself when I touched ground, but when I did touch, it was not even ground. One foot settled on gravelly earth, the other wobbled over and I came crashing down heavily on my left side. It seemed for some shattering moments that I was all pain. My head had caught the rock, my face hurt, my hand, arm and shoulder were scraped and fiercely sore. It was when I tried to move my leg, however, that I realised I was in real trouble. The pain that came from my ankle sent me sick and fainting. I don't know how long it was before I came to, lying head downwards from a ridge above a narrow valley with no track that I could see. Over a gentle-seeming mound reedy flat land began and beyond that was the goal that I wouldn't now attain, the loch with the island.

Gradually and by painful experiment I found that I wasn't in too bad shape, provided I didn't move my ankle. But without moving my ankle I wasn't likely to get very far. It was just possible that I might be able to drag myself down the hill-side to the valley bottom. But it might be better to keep to a high point from which I might see people and where I might be seen. Because I shrank in panic from the idea of moving I persuaded myself that staying put was the wiser course. The only snag was that no one came. I lay, like a rabbit caught in a trap, and scanned the valley and the more distant loch. There was a woodman, I knew, at the spruce plantations to the right, but from where I was you would never have imagined that there was a clearing with timber huts. And no one was likely to visit the island on the loch. On a summer day, perhaps, if one knew the hills well. But not at this time of year. Unless, of course, that scholarly old man with his knapsack—

I felt myself begin to stiffen up. My bruises ached, the grazed skin on my face and hands smarted. And then I felt myself growing cold. I had been over-hot from walking. There had been half an hour or so when to be cool had been pleasant. But that stage was past. Perhaps it would be better to keep up some sort of movement, to keep the circulation going, if nothing else. I edged forward in a gingerly manner and screamed out loud when the pain leapt like a live thing in my ankle. Sick again and afraid of fainting, I lay very still. I had made a thorough-going mess of things. Agnes would wonder when I didn't come back. Eventually some sort of search for me would be made. But I had told nobody where I was going, for I hadn't known. To my knowledge no one had seen me on the way. In all probability I could lie here on this ridge for days. And the ridge was high. Later mist would come down, or it would freeze. Either way the ridge would prove an inhospitable place to be. I remembered the ballad of the Twa Corbies. Thrilling, I had always thought it, about the murdered knight, his bones left

'where the wind sall blaw for evermair', made of words that rolled finely off the tongue, but not so exhilarating to think of now.

My watch had taken a knock in my fall and had stopped. I could only tell it was into the afternoon from the sun that showed fitfully through the haze. I was painfully cold now, unable to control my shivering. Every so often I made an attempt to move as though by having rested, my ankle should have mended. But the pain struck and I cowered from it, wanting to be free at least of the sick faintness. But a time came when the faintness didn't clear and I lay in a kind of helpless panic. I had not tried shouting, not believing it could be of much use, but now I tried and the effort sent me reeling senseless. I came round, wishing I could relapse into unconsciousness again, but common sense urged me to keep awake. If they were searching for me someone could pass close by without seeing me. It was up to me to keep alert. And then when daylight was fading and I had lapsed into despair that I hadn't imagined the like of, I saw someone moving in the valley. I heaved myself up and waved and yelled, and the resulting pain swamped me so that I couldn't move. When my mind had cleared and I looked again the figure had gone. Had I imagined it? The wind was rising and I thought I heard a voice. But it was illusion. There was nothing near me that lived except the sheep and the curlews.

CHAPTER SIX

I let go then. When I heard a dog barking I didn't raise my head. Soon it would melt into the freezing night air like the people I had imagined seeing and the voice I had thought I heard. Inevitably when a man's voice spoke close above me it was Keith's. It was Keith above all people in the world I wanted. I relaxed, barely feeling pain any more, and enjoyed hearing the voice I loved so well. He was speaking to me, quietly, not in any surprise or alarm. He asked me where it hurt, he told me it would be all right. I let myself drift. He was touching my face, turning my head, speaking gently. His voice came and went as though blown on the wind and there was the intermittent barking of dogs. His arms were round me now—lovely dream! I turned my face to his chest. His grip tightened. And then suddenly it was all real, and I was being lifted up and the pain in my ankle came with its white heat and everything went blank.

I have only vague memories after that, of lying slumped somewhere, and moving and jolting so that faintness came over me in waves, of voices, bright lights, people handling me none too gently, and always the annihilating pain in my ankle.

When I came to it was night. I seemed to be lying in a bed. There was a patch of shaded light nearby and I could hear someone moving about. My head ached and I was agonizingly thirsty.

'Keith,' I whispered.

Someone came from behind a screen. It was a nurse.

'Ah, so you're awake! How do you feel?'

I frowned. 'Where am I?'

'The Cottage Hospital.'

I kept carefully still. 'How did I get here?'

'I couldn't tell you that! You were brought up to us from Casualty. You've broken your ankle.'

I could believe that! I moved my leg. It didn't hurt. The nurse smiled. 'It's in plaster.'

The following day remains almost as vague. I remember nurses, a doctor, Mrs Fenton but only briefly. I asked her what had happened.

'Agnes got in touch with me when you hadn't come back by lunch-time. She thought you might have been with us. We didn't worry overmuch until into the afternoon and then I managed to contact Keith. He got the dogs on

171

your trail!'

'Rose and Cavalier?'

'He put them on your scent and they led him to you. Not without a bit of bother, I gather. They kept losing you in water.'

I had crossed the stream several times, I had even walked down part of its course on stones. 'I'm appalled to think I have given everybody so much trouble.'

'We're appalled to think you've had such an experience, my dear!'

Everybody, it seemed, wanted me to go to sleep, and that was about all I was capable of. I longed to see Keith, to thank him for what he had done, but I shrank from seeing him too and was glad that he didn't come. He sent flowers, and I lay in bed drowning, looking at them—glorious out-of-season things like freesias and roses and carnations, and I kept his card on my locker: 'Get well soon! Keith'.

It was next day when I still felt ill and my head ached and I found Elinor at my bedside that I got something of a fright.

'What on earth are *you* doing here?' I asked ungraciously.

'You've got a broken ankle and a touch of concussion and you're suffering from exposure.'

I stared at her. 'Is that all?'

'All they know about.'

'What's that supposed to mean?'

Elinor smiled. 'Don't get steamed up! When

172

you didn't come back on Saturday as planned I rang your friend Justin. I got a cock and bull story about your being all uptight and slinging him out of your house. Naturally I rang Briarybank and got your Miss Bruce.'

'Yes?'

'She told me about your accident and so I took the early morning train.'

'Oh, Elinor!'

'I can stay for a day or two. The schools are merging as I told you. They're quite pleased to be shot of me for a bit. Anyway I wanted to see where I was going to work.'

I turned my head on the pillow. Would it go on then, my plan for a school? I was too tired to think about it.

In a couple of days more I was in Briarybank. A few days later I was downstairs hobbling about with a stick. Everyone made a fuss of me. Mrs Fenton was a frequent visitor, and Sarah and Estelle. Colonel Fenton looked in on his way to the Sahara. Antonia Crawford came. She and Elinor hit it off and spent hours prowling round my kitchen premises, discussing cloakrooms and dining-space. Dave Mortimer presented himself one evening and straight away got into a wrangle with Elinor about class sizes and the number of school hours per day. I was dogged with tiredness and left them to it. I should have foreseen, from what I knew of Dave Mortimer, what the outcome would be.

173

They became fast friends, firm allies against any suggestions made by unwary outsiders, and soon I had the feeling that the outsiders included me. Try as I might, I could not get back the old enthusiasm I had had for the school. Dave brought reports of support from all over Clerkstoun, he compiled lists of names, one of children who would certainly be enrolled, another of possibles. But somehow I couldn't believe it would ever happen. I confessed something of my feeling of deadness to Elinor, who was brisk and said,

'That's natural, love, after what you've been through. Give it a few weeks!' It dawned on me that she believed I was brooding about Justin. She never mentioned him, was careful never to ask why we had quarrelled. It exasperated me out of all proportion to have her believe I cared a scrap about Justin. Only to convince her that he seldom touched my mind could have led to speculation on her part that I didn't want roused. Keith turned up one evening with Estelle. They were on their way to what Estelle called 'a farmers' hop' but which I found from the next day's 'Courier' was the Dinner and Dance of the Clerkstoun Agricultural Society, of which Keith Fenton was president. Estelle was exquisite in a peach-coloured fitting dress. Keith was exquisite too, in his way, with a midnight-blue tie and frills on his shirt front. Estelle was warm to Elinor as she had always been to me. Keith was quiet to the point of being taciturn.

'So that's your lord of the manor!' Elinor remarked when they had gone. I had the feeling she wasn't overly impressed.

Elinor went back to Manchester at the week-end, driven to her train in Edinburgh by Dave Mortimer and his brood.

Ungraciously I felt glad to be on my own again in my house. In all sorts of ways everything seemed to have been taken out of my hands. I limped about, studying the rooms, trying to visualise them as class-rooms. I went into the garden, well wrapped-up at Agnes's insistence, and hobbled as far as the stream. Sometimes I met up with old Jessie Bruce.

'I'm weel pleased,' she told me one day, 'that ye've got rid o' that wee bit English mannie!'

Sarah dropped in regularly to see me. Somehow she seemed to have lost something of her old ebullience and sparkle. Having been accused of interference by Keith, I hesitated to enquire too closely about her own plans. A time came, however, when it would have seemed odd not to.

'Old Keith's a reformed character,' she said. 'He's spent several evenings with me going over university brochures, cross-questioning me and double-checking, and deciding in the end that I might fill up an UCCA form.'

'And have you?'

175

'Oh yes. For anthropology. Got it off to my old school for the Headmistress's report. Meanwhile I'm going to do a secretarial course, starting after Christmas.'

'In Clerkstoun?'

'London. Mummy has postponed the family visits until the New Year. I'll go down with her and stay with one of my aunts, or perhaps with each in turn in case they get jealous!'

'Will you like being in London?'

'Not much. But it will be good to get out of Fenton.'

'Sarah!' I stared at her.

'I can't explain. They don't tell me anything. But there's an atmosphere. Estelle and Keith are hand in glove and at each other's throats, all at the same time, if you can see what I mean.'

I could see.

'And Mummy just rides it out, playing at being calm and placid. Only I know her too well. She's worried.'

Once or twice she tried to persuade me to go over to Fenton House for tea. 'You're looking peaky,' she would say. 'You need a change of scene!'

But I could not risk meeting Keith. Not yet. I'd have to get back to Manchester for a stint, distance myself from what had happened. I made the excuse that I didn't feel up to it, but she must have put her own construction on what I said, for one morning she rang.

176

'I'll collect you this afternoon, Lucy. You could manage in the Landrover if I gave you a leg up? Keith's going off to London on business and Estelle is driving him to Edinburgh.'

I agreed and was ready when she called for me soon after two. The day had suddenly turned bitterly cold. The ground was iron-hard with frost. Icicles formed from the house eaves. The sky was tawny-coloured with the snow that was to fall.

'I hate this sort of day.' Sarah sat tense, prepared for ice on the road. 'Just think of Dad sweltering in the Sahara!'

'Have you heard from him?'

'Oh yes! He's a smashing letter-writer. He has written a couple of travel books, did you know?'

'I didn't know.'

'He lectures too. Got the gift of the gab!'

I watched her young face, unusually serious. She was missing her father, needing him rather badly with those under-currents she had spoken of in Fenton House. She took the drive carefully and I was grateful, remembering the pot-holes. It was good to be out of the confines of Briarybank. Here in the wide parklands was a sense of space. We rounded the tree mass and the shrubbery. The family car was standing at the front door.

'They haven't left *yet*!' Sarah spoke out of exasperation.

I sat back in my seat. If only I had taken longer to get ready!

Sarah drew up by the conservatory. 'Go along in,' she said. 'I must check that Parsifal has enough straw. I was out with him just before lunch and he had a good rub-down afterwards. But it's got so much colder. The old boy mustn't get a chill.'

Was she making an excuse, I wondered, not to see Keith and Estelle? She had obviously said her goodbyes already. I would have followed her to the stables gladly, but the yards were cobbled and difficult for me to walk on. It was much too cold to stand about. I let myself into the conservatory, enjoying the impact of warmth fragrant with plants. There were exciting things coming along for Christmas, azaleas in pots, some fine poinsettias and a selection of hyacinths in bowls, the bulbs at different stages of growth. I was examining a delicate cyclamen when I heard footsteps in the hall, a woman's and a man's. Keith and Estelle must just be going. Then Keith spoke quite near the conservatory door.

'With the roads as they are I just can't have you driving me to Edinburgh and coming back on your own after dark!'

'My gallant Keith!' I heard Estelle's gurgling laugh.

'And Heaven knows,' he said, 'what conditions will be like when I get back from

London—'

'So you drive yourself up, park the car and save petrol on a double journey!'

'Right!'

'Good points, both! But not really why you want to drive yourself! You want clear of me, don't you?'

'*Estelle!*'

I heard pain and entreaty in his voice and wondered where I could go to avoid eavesdropping.

'You know I'd nag until the very last minute, until the train was pulling out of Waverley. Keith—'

'My dear,' he said, 'we have been over this already.'

I could imagine her close to him, looking up into his face, Keith looking down at her, that line drawn in his cheek—

'I must go, and clinch this deal. There may never be an offer like it again!'

'But how *can* you sell Fenton House?'

My head came up sharply from the cyclamen. I hadn't expected this!

'By putting my signature on the nice lawyer man's documents!'

'Stop teasing, Keith!'

'I'm sorry, but I've told you! I'm broke. I can't keep up this house and maintain the estate. I've never cared for this house. It's a vulgar ostentatious pile. If Alba Hotels think

179

they can make a go of it, good luck to them! And I'll put the money into the land where it's needed—'

'Which would have been fine if you could have bought up Briarybank. As it is, what about the family seat?'

'Estelle, don't be so feudal! Mother and Dad wouldn't come here if there wasn't this mausoleum of a place to be filled up somehow. Sarah's planning a life of her own—'

'And you?'

'Well, there's that house the factor had when we could afford a factor—'

'A glorified cottage!'

'Which would suit me well enough.'

'And all the treasures? The pictures and the books and the furniture?'

'What we don't want to part with we can distribute somehow—'

'Keith, *there is another way!*'

'*No!*'

I heard his footsteps rapid on the floor. 'I'm going to miss that train!'

'Fine! Miss the damn' train! Go and see Antonia! They've got money to rejuvenate twenty estates. Old Crawford would be tickled pink to have his daughter marry into a family like ours—'

'A family like ours!' He gave a strangled laugh. 'It just happens I don't *love* Antonia!'

'Love! My mother went for love and we all

180

know where that got her! You *like* Antonia, she likes you. That can be a better basis for marriage than love!'

'I won't accept that.'

'You can't afford not to!'

He said, 'This isn't France!'

'Keith, if you don't marry Antonia, she'll be snapped up by that opera-singing lawyer. I've worked like crazy to divert him and throw you and Antonia together—but *he* knows a good thing when he sees it! *He* can use his head!'

'Unhand me, cousin! I'm going!'

'That's your last word on it?'

'Positively.'

There was a pause. Now I was straining unashamedly to hear.

Estelle said, 'All right, then. If you won't go after Antonia Crawford, marry Lucy Lorimer. That way you'd retrieve Briarybank! Without buying it!'

I recoiled, clutching at the metal column for support. I heard Keith's voice. It was angry now. 'For God's sake!' Faintness came over me. The plant scents, sickly sweet, were stifling. I must have fresh air. Stumbling for the door, I lurched into Sarah.

'Lucy, you look ghastly! Darling, what's wrong?'

I leant against the open door, drawing the cutting cold into my lungs. 'Sorry,' I whispered. 'Not feeling too good. Could you be

181

an angel and take me home?'

'Come into the house.'

'No, please! I want to go home.'

She helped me into the Landrover. I sat with my face against the window glass. The car that Keith would drive to Edinburgh was still at the front door.

'I shouldn't have persuaded you to come out,' she said. 'It was too soon for you in this awful cold.'

'No. It was just—' I drew a deep breath and steadied myself. I mustn't distress her. She had worries enough, and a shock coming. Obviously nobody had had the courage to tell her. She had sensed crisis, misinterpreting the symptoms as one does. 'What happened was, I jarred my foot. The pain made me all groggy.'

'Oh, Lucy!'

At Briarybank I had to make a show of limping into the house. Agnes came out of the kitchen and the two of them fussed over me. The last thing I wanted was that they should insist on contacting the doctor.

'It's really all right,' I said. 'I know what caused it. I forgot about the wretched ankle and stepped down on it with all my weight. There's no harm done.'

They wanted me to go upstairs, but agreed to my resting in the study. Inevitably Agnes made tea. Sarah said,

'Just relax. I'll stay with you.'

182

'There's no need!' I sipped the hot tea. Desperate to be alone I cast about in my mind for ways of persuading her to go.

'Was Parsifal all right?' I asked.

'I gave him some extra straw.'

I noticed some flakes of snow idling down from the lowering sky. 'You'd better get back before the road ices up, Sarah. Your mother is bound to be wondering where you've got to.'

'Gosh, yes! I'll phone her—'

'Look, my dear, I really feel like sleeping.'

She got up from the floor beside my chair, her fair hair falling over her face. 'Of course,' she said. 'I'll ring this evening to see how you are. 'Bye for now.'

She waved to me from the door, her piquant little face quenched of its vitality. She knew I was sending her away and she didn't know why.

''Bye!' I said, and managed to smile. Not 'Bye for now. 'Bye for always.

I waited until I heard the Landrover move down the drive and then I limped to the desk.

'Dear Sarah,' I wrote, 'When you get this you will be surprised to hear that I have left. I had some news today which upset me. That is probably why I wasn't feeling so good. I have to get back to Manchester. You will be hearing that after all I shall not be staying on in Briarybank. I should like to think that maybe one day you will! I shall never forget all your great kindness to me. I hope everything works out for you as you would wish. With my love, Lucy.'

After that I wrote once again to Mr Macdonald, that dry old lawyer in Edinburgh, informing him that I had looked into the question of turning Briarybank into a school as I had said I would in my earlier letter and had come to the conclusion that the plan was not practicable. I was therefore instructing him to undertake the sale of the property on my behalf, not by auction, however, but through the alternative method of advertising and inviting offers. I asked that all correspondence should be directed to my Manchester address.

The next letter was to Dave Mortimer. I thanked him for his help and encouragement on the school project. 'I have given the matter a lot of thought during my recent period of enforced inactivity and have come reluctantly to the conclusion that while I am sure it could be done, I am not the person to do it. I am more sorry than I can say about taking up so much of your time and disappointing you now. However I am sure that some of the ideas you have been evolving these last few weeks will be given concrete form elsewhere and (who knows?) before too long!'

I had just taken up the paper for the last and most difficult letter when Agnes came in. She scrutinised me and nodded.

'You're looking better.'

'Am I, Agnes? Then it must be because I've taken a decision.'

'And what might that be?'

'I must get back to Manchester tomorrow.'

'Manchester! The morn? You're bletherin', girl!'

Since we had been set on the way to friendship she tended to slip more into vernacular. 'Why would you be wanting to do that? Look at the weather!' Snow was still drifting past the window. 'And you not all that well!'

'I'm well enough, Agnes. Something has cropped up—'

'Oh, aye?' She pursed her mouth and the dour look was back that I had known in the early days. 'I didna bring in the letters this morning—' It wasn't a statement so much as a question, an opening for me to give some explanation. I tried a casual smile but it couldn't have been very convincing.

'Well,' she said, 'it's not for me to say what you should do or shouldna do. What would you like for your supper? There's a nice bit o' fish—'

I said fish would be lovely with some of her excellent tartare sauce. But blandishment got me nowhere. There was none of the softening in her face or manner that I had come to expect and find. She rearranged a cushion and pulled the rug straight.

185

'What time did you plan on leaving?'

'I'll order a taxi for nine in the morning. That should get me to the bus in time.'

'Just as you say. And you won't know when you will be coming back?'

'I'll write, Agnes.' I could not bring myself to speak the words that I had been able to put down for the others on paper.

She went out, her back held stiff. I half-rose in protest. *Agnes, no! Don't let's part like this! We're friends.* And then in chilled dismay I realised what it must be that she was thinking. That I had had word from Justin. And that, having heard from him, the quarrel made up, I couldn't wait to rush back to him. For it had been from the moment of my outburst against Justin that she had thawed towards me, made me welcome. I went to the window, seared with the pain of knowing my motives so thoroughly misunderstood. But did it matter? Wasn't it made easier this way? I would be writing to Agnes, telling her that Briarybank was going up for sale and that I wouldn't be back. She would let me drop, then, into the pool of her memory and I wouldn't be talked of again. Whatever she thought, however disappointed she might feel personally, she would never gossip about me. She would not discuss me even with her mother. I was Miss Lorimer and she had her loyalty.

I came back to the desk and the last letter.

186

'Dear Keith,' I wrote and sat for a long time, looking at his name. I love you more than I ever thought I should be able to love anyone. Your problems are quite other than I imagined. Your land is in jeopardy, those fields and hills and woods you love. You have a buyer for the splendid house you can't afford to keep up. Sell it, my dearest, and with a fraction of the money you get, buy Briarybank. Briarybank, the original home of the Fentons, where portraits of your ancestors still hang on the walls. Buy Briarybank, since I know you would not take it from me—although it would be such a happiness for me to give it—buy it, live in it, my darling, restore your estate and be happy.

'I am writing to let you know that after a great deal of thought I have decided that I cannot undertake the task of turning Briarybank into a school. That being so, I am unable to keep it up and I have instructed Mr Macdonald, the family solicitor in Edinburgh, to put it on the market. I have gathered that you might be interested in acquiring the property and as our families have been acquainted for a long time I shall make it known to my lawyer that, subject to your offering a fair price, you may have the first refusal. I should like to thank you and all the family for your great kindness to me during my visit to Briarybank. Yours, Lucy Lorimer.'

I sealed the letters and carried them upstairs.

I packed my case, clearing the Yellow Room of all traces of my occupation. Flowers that people had sent me were withering. Some freesias from Keith's bouquet were still in a vase beside my bed. They had dried and the fragrance had gone. Should I take one, press it in a book, keep it as my sole memento of him? I emptied all the vases, wrapped the flowers in newspaper and carried them downstairs to the waste-bin. I brought down the vases and washed them out. I would need no memento of Keith. I wasn't likely to forget him. If only I could hope that I might!

I ate the supper that Agnes brought me. There was no pause tonight for the nearest she ever came to a chat. In due course Sarah rang. She sounded distant almost as though I had already been gone for some time. There was so much I would have wanted to say to her, but I could risk nothing. When she rang off I went upstairs to bed.

I awoke next morning to a silent world. Snow lay deep on the hills, the garden, on the roofs, on every branch. The sky was clear. The sun was brilliant, glinting gold on the snow, casting long blue shadows from the house and the trees and in every wheel-rut. Agnes served breakfast in the kitchen. 'Maybe you'll not get through.'

Maybe I wouldn't! I ate my porridge slowly, the last of hers I would have, and allowed myself to dream. I saw myself marooned in a

188

snow-drift between Briarybank and Clerkstoun. We would be stuck for hours. Long enough for Keith to get back from London and come riding up on his horse and dig me out. But he couldn't be back from London until late that night or the following morning. Or perhaps he hadn't got to London at all! The main line could be closed. Perhaps even now he was in Edinburgh waiting for the line to open and I'd get to Edinburgh and come face to face with him in Waverley Station!

Agnes brought in the mail—a letter with a Manchester post-mark. It was from Elinor, but Agnes couldn't know the handwriting.

'The post-man says the roads are passable.'

My dream went. Elinor's letter was all enthusiasm for the school, with an account of some new ideas Dave had sent her. I wasn't looking forward to the session I would be having with her that evening. And then the taxi was at the door. The driver took my suitcase. Agnes armed me over the packed snow on the drive. I was so occupied with manipulating my ankle in its casing of plaster and stowing away my grandfather's walking-stick that there was time for no more than a quick goodbye to Agnes and a blurred glance at the front of my beloved house before the taxi was sweeping round the overgrown hollies. I had my letters ready in my hand-bag. The taxi-driver stopped by the post office, got stamps for me. I watched him drop the letters into the yawning post-box.

The bus run over the Lowland Hills had its moments of excitement. In Edinburgh, however, and all along the Lothian shore, as I could see coming down over Soutra, there was not a vestige of snow. It was easier travelling with a suitcase and a stick and a foot in plaster than I had imagined. Men were gallant. Without undue wear on the nerves I eventually was settled into the Manchester train. Slowly we pulled out under the bastions of the Castle rock, and I felt as heavy-hearted as though I were leaving my home-land.

Leaning back, with eyes closed, I felt the ease of being really alone at last. I understood it all now, Keith's distress at my decision to keep the modest old Fenton home that he had been planning to buy when he could dispose of Fenton House, the burden of strain under which he had been living. No wonder Sarah had not had the interest and attention from him that she had been used to! Now, too, I understood Estelle. Half-French and caring passionately about family—not least because her mother had flouted it—she had done her best to manipulate Keith into marrying money. Estelle had not supported him in wanting to sell Fenton House and retrench in Briarybank. She had seen the Crawfords supplying the money to keep up the more splendid house out of pride in having gained a place in an old family. I doubted if

Antonia, from what I had seen of her, was a woman of deep feelings, but she would have been happy enough to marry Keith. Bitterly I thought, what woman wouldn't? But Keith didn't love her! And as for Estelle's last words, her throw-away last-resort suggestion—My cheeks burned at the memory of Keith's cry of outrage.

Once more in my mind I went over their exchange. Were they in love with each other, he wanting against common sense to marry Estelle and live in a cottage if need be; she, the realist, putting family fortunes first, ready to let go love that had proved a snare to her mother? Neither way would he find happiness.

In Manchester it was raining. As in Edinburgh the sight of a girl with a foot in plaster brought out the gallantry in everyone I encountered. I was at the flat in no time. Mercifully Elinor was still at school and I had time to unpack, change, get myself organised.

As I had imagined she had a shock when she saw me and another when I told her I was selling Briarybank.

'But, Lucy, why? The school was a good idea. And a lot of people put a lot of thought into how it could be organised!' She was even more heated and vexed than I had anticipated, and as she talked on I began to see why. She and Dave Mortimer—and now, if there was to be no school—What a mess I had made from

191

start to finish! I had hampered Keith, giving him worry and distress. I had done damage to Elinor. There was nothing I could say beyond the old formula. 'It's all too much. I can't go on with it!'

'You aren't the one who would be doing the most of it,' she retorted. 'Do you really have to decide now, when you've just been ill? Leave it for a week or two, take time to think about it.'

'I have thought about it, Elinor. The decision has been made.'

'If changing your instructions to the lawyer is what's worrying you, there's nothing to changing your instructions again!'

An echo of what Justin had said! And as if she had been seeing the thoughts in my mind she said, 'It's Justin, I suppose?'

I stared at her stupidly.

'He never wanted you to keep the house. He wanted you to sell it, to have the lolly in your hand. And he's persuaded you, has he? Oh, heavens, I thought you had more sense!'

She turned away from the fireplace where she had been leaning on the mantelpiece. I sat on in my chair screwing my hands together as if to tighten control on my tongue. I could not, must not, divulge anything of the truth. No one should ever know from me how things were with Keith's estate. If by letting everyone think I was selling my house to please Justin I could keep them off the scent, it was worth it.

There was a coolness between us all that evening and on the Thursday morning. Elinor is not one to indulge in sulks or resentful silences but she does not suffer fools gladly and believing me to be a thorough-going fool, she saw no reason why she should make pretence that she thought otherwise. For my part, exhausted from the emotional turmoil of the last days and aching with longing for an impossible might-have-been, I indulged in self-pity at being misunderstood by the friend who should have given me support.

Elinor went in late to her school. They appeared to be working some sort of shift system. The hours dragged interminably. Rain spattered the window panes. At three in the afternoon darkness began to fall. I stood by the window looking down the row of red brick semis and remembered my Shining Hill. Where would Keith be now? Back from London? Had he closed the deal turning Fenton House into a hotel? I wondered when he would break the news to Sarah and how she would take it.

At two minutes past six the telephone rang, sending my nerves thrilling. Elinor answered and I heard her say, 'Dave!'

I sank back into my chair. Who had I imagined it might be, for heaven's sake? *He* wouldn't ring. In due course I would probably have a letter in answer to mine, couched in terms as formal as mine had been. I began to hear something of what Elinor was saying: 'Disappointed, of course . . . She's feeling badly under the weather . . . We just have to respect her decision . . .' There was a closing of ranks, anyway, no disloyalty! And then suddenly the tone of her voice changed. There was a new quickening interest, an excitement. She wasn't doing much of the talking, only an occasional, 'Yes?' and 'You think you might?' The call went on for longer than I would have expected from that dour thrifty Scot. When Elinor came off the phone her colour was high and her eyes sparkling.

'Lucy, you'll never guess!'

I was puzzled and longing to hear and said testily,

'Obviously not!'

'Dave is going to make *his* house into a nursery school!'

'*His* house?'

'It's quite roomy, on the road that runs under the big houses on the hill. He has had the idea before, in a kind of a way. And now after all the thinking that was done over Briarybank he's really got the bit between his teeth. He'd had a letter from you this morning.'

'Yes.'

'He was terribly disappointed at first. Was quite mad with you all day, he said. He rang Mr Fenton. He had been away in London—'

My heart was thudding. How had Keith

194

reacted?

'He had been very surprised too.'

'Really?' Was that all?

'*And*—' Elinor took up her favourite stance by the fire—'Dave has suggested that I might like to run the school for him! With an assistant, of course. We could get a local girl.'

I looked at her bright face and noticed how she avoided meeting my eyes. His suggestion meant more than that she should run a nursery school. I knew that and she knew that and I was happy that she was happy. Jealous, too. It would work well. They would be a match for each other, straight-speaking, uncompromising, each with an individual sense of humour. She would mother his children and eventually take the place in his heart of that selfless little wife he had loved so much.

'Well, that's great!' I said. 'Let's drink to it, shall we? The Dave-Elinor School!'

I tried hard to be cheerful that evening, but Elinor was not deceived. I caught her watching me. Once or twice the phone rang and each time irrationally my stupid heart leapt and I knew my colour changed. In the morning I was up early to catch the post, but there was nothing for me. Elinor noticed that too, and from her own happiness tried to speak to me. But I pretended not to understand and turned her words away. She was not due to leave the house until eleven and by ten o'clock I could stand it no longer.

'I'm going round to Gatskill Primary,' I told her, 'to see how my infants are getting on.'

'But you can't cope with buses.'

'Oh yes, I can. The plaster should come off next week. It's more than time I was getting back to work.'

She did not try to dissuade me. It was a clear morning, with wintry sunshine lying on the pavements and warming the house bricks to a rich ruby red. I walked most of the way, using my stick for support, taking the bus only for the last few stops. Walking in the fresh air helped me to think. Dave's plan to turn his own house into the nursery school he wanted for Clerkstoun and the special place he had for Elinor in those plans released me from any guilt I had been feeling towards her. Keith I had tried to help in the only way I knew. Now I could think of myself. With Elinor gone north there was no reason for my staying in Manchester. In fact it would be as well to get away. New scenes, new faces, that was what they prescribed for heart-break, wasn't it? I would work out my notice at Gatskill and keep an eye open for another job. So often I had noticed ads for girls to take charge of children in exotic spots—Athens, Rome, Cairo, the Bahamas—surely in such a place a girl would meet exciting people. I let my imagination run on: in the rich family who employed me there would be a younger brother, handsome, a bit of a lad, but with a heart in the right place. I imagined a swarthy Greek, a dark-eyed Roman. In Cairo—I drew the line at hopes of a sheik. And then I thought of Keith and the bright images fell to dust—like the particles that the wind lifted from the gutter to gain a moment's magic glinting in the sunlight.

I had a warmer reception at the school than I had expected. After a chat with the headmistress I went along to see my class. They were thrilled with my plaster and those who could write, inscribed their names on it in coloured crayon. They wanted to know all about my accident and I told them about the wild country where all you could see for miles were birds and sheep.

It was nearly twelve when I got back and let myself into the flat. The little expedition had been more of an effort than I liked to admit. I was tired. The rest of the day stretched ahead of me empty. The pleasure I had had from seeing the children was seeping away. How to fill the hours? I went into the living-room. Keith faced me across the floor.

Caught completely off-balance, physically faint for a moment, I grasped the back of a chair and let it take my sagging weight.

'Miss Braidwood let me in,' he said.

'Oh yes, of course.' I could not bring myself to look at him, nor to ask him why he had come.

He said, 'I had your letter.'

I bent my head. I should offer him coffee, but I simply had not the strength. 'Won't you sit down?'

He remained where he was, standing against the window, as though he hadn't heard. Elinor must have put the gas fire on for him. Its warmth was reaching me now, helping me to steady up.

He said, 'Why did you change your mind about keeping on Briarybank?'

'I explained in my letter. I wrote to Dave Mortimer too.'

'He told me.'

'It was just going to be all too much.'

'It seemed to me when I read your letter that your decision had been reached rather too suddenly.'

'It wasn't sudden. I had plenty of time to think about it when I was convalescing.'

'Dave and Elinor were behind you. Other people too. I'm afraid,' he said, 'you haven't convinced me.'

I looked at him now. His face had a formal look, he was showing the front he would present to timber merchants and agents buying houses for hotels. He wasn't a friend.

A spurt of irritation helped me to shrug. 'Do I have to?'

'Before I consider your proposition, yes.'

'Why else should I consider selling the house?'

'That's what I want to find out.'

'I don't want to be rude, but is it your business?'

He permitted himself a wry smile. 'It could be.'

Suddenly, desperately, I wanted him to go. He said, 'Sit down in that chair, instead of hugging the back of it! You're passing out on your feet. You shouldn't be roaming round the country like this! You aren't fit.'

I slipped round the chair and sank into it.

'I may say Agnes copped it when I found she'd let you go.'

'That wasn't fair! Agnes could not have stopped me.'

'Poor soul, she wanted to. Lucy, I'd like a straight answer to one or two questions. Justin came up for you but you didn't go back with him. Agnes is loyalty personified but I've known her all my life and I can read her like a book. There was a quarrel, I think? It wasn't because of me, was it?'

Oh no, Keith Fenton, you needn't have any fear of being involved!

'About *you*?'

My apparent scorn stung him and he reddened. 'I'm sorry. I had to know.' He half-turned at the window and fiddled with the catch. 'Agnes formed the impression that you

199

and he have now made it up? Elinor too, I gather—'

I sprang to my feet. 'What possible right have you got to cross-question me about my private affairs? Or people to gossip? I fail to see what this has to do with my selling Briarybank!'

'Your friends don't gossip, Lucy. They care for you. If Justin's advice was to turn your property into capital—'

'Justin Wain has nothing in the world to do with my selling my property! I have had no contact with Justin Wain since I sent him out of Briarybank, nor do I wish to!'

He moved in from the window so that we stood a couple of yards apart. 'Then if it isn't because of Justin why the sudden change of heart? Why this sudden decision to sell?'

His eyes were hard and bright and I knew I had walked into his trap. He said, 'I've talked to Sarah and to Agnes, pieced together exactly what happened on Tuesday afternoon when I was leaving for London. Sarah left you to go into the house while she checked up on Parsifal. I suggest that from the conservatory you heard a conversation I had with Estelle?'

Hunching away from him I leant my arms along the mantelpiece.

'And if I did?'

I saw him spread his hands as his half-French cousin might have done. 'I can't have you selling your house out of some noble impulse to

200

save the Fenton name.'

'It wasn't quite like that.'

'How was it, Lucy?'

I dropped my head on my arms. 'I simply don't want to live there any more.'

'Don't you?'

'Have you sold Fenton House?'

'I have.'

'And you'll live in a cottage on the estate?'

'I shan't mind that.'

'But Estelle will mind.'

'Too bad for Estelle! She'll be off to Paris as soon as the show is over to her dashing Henri.'

I prised myself from the mantelpiece. *'Henri?'*

'A very dishy dress designer who would have preferred Estelle plus a handsome family home in the background, but will probably settle for her without it.'

'And you don't mind?'

'Me?' His eyes seemed to bore into my mind. Then he drew a sharp breath. 'You didn't imagine I've been harbouring a grand passion for Estelle?' He began to laugh and my cheeks flamed. Then he stopped. 'It seems we're quits. I was sure your heart had been snared by your—' He broke off on the point of saying something derogatory and I finished for him '—wee bit mannie!'

We were both laughing then. 'Dear Agnes,' he said. 'Or was that Jessie? Let's hope that

201

whoever buys Briarybank will let them stay on!'

'But *you* are buying Briarybank!'

'No.'

I gazed up into his face. It was stern again, but no longer shut against me. His eyes were very tender.

'Bless you for what you tried to do, Lucy.' He took my hands in both of his. 'You must sell or keep your house as you think best.'

He could never buy Briarybank because he knew why I was offering it for sale. Just as he could never ask me to marry him, even if he loved me. I stood very still, my hands in his. What was my woman's pride at a moment like this? He could never speak. Only I could.

I bent my head low. 'Keith,' I whispered, 'you do know, don't you, why I decided to sell? *Really* why. You know what I feel for you—'

I felt a trembling go through his body. I forced myself to say the words, 'We could marry.'

'And have everybody in Clerkstoun saying I had married you to get your house and save my face!'

I stepped back from him, drawing away my hands. Later when he had gone there would be time for the tears that ached in my throat. 'What other people say matters more than how I feel! So I've had my answer?'

'*No!*'

I was in his arms then, crushed against him

202

so that I could scarcely breathe.

'Don't torture me, Lucy! How can you have any doubt about how I feel for you? Right from the start I've loved you and wanted you! I made it plain enough—that day on the island—' His cheek pressed mine. *'But what was I to do? What can I do now?'*

Keith loved me. Nothing else in the world mattered. We would live in Briarybank, with the portrait of my knight, his ancestor, at the head of the stairs. I turned my lips to his.

'My darling,' I whispered, 'take me home soon!'

Photoset, printed and bound in Great Britain by REDWOOD PRESS LIMITED, Melksham, Wiltshire